Both Sides of the Sun

"Debut Poems by Jade Renae"

PERSIA MCLEOD

authorHOUSE

AuthorHouse™
1663 Liberty Drive
Bloomington, IN 47403
www.authorhouse.com
Phone: 1 (800) 839-8640

© 2016 Persia McLeod. All rights reserved.

No part of this book may be reproduced, stored in a retrieval system, or transmitted by any means without the written permission of the author.

This is a work of fiction. All of the characters, names, incidents, organizations, and dialogue in this novel are either the products of the author's imagination or are used fictitiously.

Published by AuthorHouse August 27, 2016

ISBN: 978-1-4817-3398-4 (sc)
ISBN: 978-1-4817-3399-1 (e)

Library of Congress Control Number: 2016913723

Print information available on the last page.

Any people depicted in stock imagery provided by Thinkstock are models, and such images are being used for illustrative purposes only. Certain stock imagery © Thinkstock.

This book is printed on acid-free paper.

Because of the dynamic nature of the Internet, any web addresses or links contained in this book may have changed since publication and may no longer be valid. The views expressed in this work are solely those of the author and do not necessarily reflect the views of the publisher, and the publisher hereby disclaims any responsibility for them.

Introduction

A story of a young woman, who started out with convictions but not of her own by which she was born too. She grew into a bully to be overwhelmed by atmosphere. It wasn't poverty that held her back but emotional restrictions. Missing parents, but she had strong extended family. Follow her through a journey that no one expected of her but determination led her to strength and confidence of what she knew she didn't want her life to be.

Soulful Upbringing

Born in NJ in the 70's, under the wrath of Drugs and Booze. Only 10 months old left to fend for myself. A call in the night the baby is restless for almost 3 days. On arrival there was the stink of 8 babies. Dirty diaper, snotty nose, and naturally hungry for days. This was just the start of a life that made me strong and independent. Janet was young, foolish and selfish. She was married in an abusive relationship and found her peace in her heroin. As in most relationships the responsibility laid in her hands as the responsible parent. Except, responsibility wasn't in her vocabulary. A young child was only a disturbance of her life.

There is always blame without an understanding on the facts. Janet lived in a suburban area with very responsible parents. Father was working for Merck Pharmaceutical in Rahway, NJ and Mother was a seamstress/presser at a dress shop of Linden, NJ. She was taught in the church with very strict discipline but it did her no good as an adult. She was always special in what she felt was right for her. Again the selfish ways of her life led her to the lifestyle she followed. Her career title was a "Booster" kinder word for thief that gets paid amongst the neighborhood for poultry foods, clothing, electronics or anything that can be stolen and sold. So where does the blame go for this young adult starting a family.

The circumstance of one's life is chosen as an adult no matter your background or past. As a child you're taught by many as many as you will listen too. You are never too old to listen to an ole folk story of the wise. Growing up you may think here they go with those "When I was…" stories. That story may just be the one to open your eyes to a path you don't want to travel. A wise word is to always have an ear for the elderly or the knowledgeable. I took this advice for myself after a long journey of hitting the walls head first. Let me tell you a little about the events that led to my journey.

I grew up in suburban area of NJ and felt after being adapted to my grandparents I was given what you may call a fair chance. I think it was the nightmares of my weekend visits with Mom that portioned most of my behavior issues that started early. I fought on a daily basis with my anger of why I couldn't have my mother be a parent to me.

Of course it was everybody faults except hers to me. She dressed me, taught me very bad habits to fight and that life is what you take not what you make it. I had a bad attitude and no respect for my elders. I must say that she told me too, but it was a part of my blame game not to respect my maternal grandmother.

My grandmother, the most caring, loving respected woman you could ever meet. She had style, class and loved everyone. Love was not missing in my life she loved me more than anyone could. She gave me until giving was unheard of. I never had to earn anything, just ask. I was well dressed, well educated, and always had cash. Learned early that I just have to get from my grandmother and make the rest follow.

The other option was to take as my mother taught me. Fighting was a part of life to avoid dealing with the anger I had inside for the issues I hated to face. My mother putting the needle in her arm, the nodding off she went through and the fact my siblings weren't with me. Why I had to live with grandparents? While I didn't know where my mother was when incarcerated the "big secret"!

I spent many travels back and forth down the roads to see my mother in prison. I think she was a better mother then than ever. I had gotten knitted sweaters, gloves, and scarves. There was also a craft class we were in with my mother during our visits. I had hoped that the bond we created inside would be enforced when she returned home. Unfortunately, that's not how that story ended. The most bonding time I spent with my mother was from the inside, which is where all my feelings stood.

I had excluded my father memories into my life since he passed when I was two. Passed, sounds so gently but gentle wasn't what he stood for to put lightly. My father was a veteran of the Marines and loved his career and his family. He was the second oldest male of his family and feared by most of his peers. Angry, violent but respected, especially by the ladies.

I decided to be sure to submit this part regarding my father's life since many times we excuse them as they make excuses for themselves as men do. My father was high strung and very strong in his opinion. I know all of this only from stories and character that was built in my head of my father. He loved me I know that I prayed for him to tell me all the time from his beyond gates. I felt that his presence should have been near after all I was his baby girl.

I think his death had a terrible hold over my mother although he was, let's say rough with her, he was her husband. They had some weird attraction he was 8 years older and she loved the bad boy in him. Just a guess on how I tend to wonder off in thought these days in regards to men.

I had been blessed with my Father's side of the family to teach me unity and togetherness. We did everything together. Camping, hiking, walking trails, picnics, and all the family outings I can think of we did. It gave me that sense of family and how it should be. It also let me know that unity is how things are really accomplished.

My fraternal grandmother gave me the strong backbone that I strive off of. She had the will of an iron skillet. Grandma raised 14 children while my grandfather was away on ship. I learned respect, understanding and communication through her with her teachings and way of life. She was strong in "Jesus" and walked as an angel, she was my rock, shield, hope and motivation. I only wish her life was distilled within my soul so I can walk her path. I took on her feisty side that didn't take any mess as she passed it to my father.

I grew up in a small 10-block town of a small state but the life I lived was as big as a rough-rocking city. I was always missing the security that I needed to grow that only a mother/parent can give. Although, unlike.... most I don't take my shortcomings as an excuse for screwing up my life. As an adult you know what was, could have, or should have been is not where things are. You make it happen by the tools you were given and learn from the mistakes of your elders and grow strong in the things that are much clearer to life expectations.

There are many stories like mine so I won't bore you with the sssssoooo....soooo...what! Here is where my difference lies. I was a tomboy who loved to be tough, just my exterior to escape life's rough road. I learned that rough road early. Always took education as a plus, smart to death, pretty to the eye, but a wall higher in my heart that love couldn't even break. I always prayed to my father to be a part of my life. Yes, I knew he was deceased but something in my mind said he was with me and I felt him.

I never wanted to give up on that hope. Needed that strong figure to say no to me when I needed and the hand to back at me with conviction. I took every dare there was to feel dominant to all those around me. I liked the sweet, soft things that make you feel, look and play girly. No one but those close was to know that. I liked to fight, hang out with the guys, challenge them, and out do them. It strengthened my outlook on what boys to men do and how they react. So I grew up thinking they were all alike and fun to be around. At the age of 11 I started getting curious but felt it was something terribly wrong with me.

This was the time I started feeling to hang with the girls and see what they do. It was always boy crazy feigns around me. Thirteen as I started to get the picture of all it meant I was snatched from out of my environment.

My mother as I always said kidnapped me from a home to chaos and I was now forced to grow another personality around strangers and out of state. I met my currently best friend Kita. I was now starting to be reared up in the housing authority as new meat to the dogs in heat. I also became Ms. Prissy, the one of mystery, wonder and distinctive measures of fitting in. Kita was the one that was already in the game and found me to be the interesting one that actually befriended her in total ahhh, which she was able to connect with another female.

Fortunately, she was the one to easily let me see being a tomboy in Jersey didn't help me characterize the boys and men of good nature or just jiving for the image they wanted to portray of the dirty south. I wanted so much to be grown, and do what I wanted to do, by 16 I was bored and out of control.

Let's see let's start with "Youngblood" that's what they called him. Tall, dark, handsome and full of all the jive there is to live by. Vulnerable to wanting to fit in, he preyed upon me and I fell for it. It (the vibe…) had me tripping. I didn't want to come home, stayed out all night. Knowing Janet (my mother) did not play that!

I didn't care because that vibe had me sprung. Janet came to the house knocking at the door and I just ignored the calls. When I got ready I went home all nonchalant walking past all at my porch. Good morning, like I was supposed to be coming in at 11:00am after not being seen all night at 13 yrs old!

That was the day Janet said she was going to whoop the dailax out of me. She stormed up the stairs after me, went to go swigging bare hands as she does. I stood there with heart of a warrior, not budging or even attempting to show emotions never alone to cry. Then she turned and said to me you know what forget hurting myself, you will have a child soon.

Timeless Love

It's in the warmth of your touch
The beauty in your eyes that this smile
This love
No one can take away
Not this of mine
In the rhythm of your voice
The strength shown in your work
The embrace of your character
I am all loved..no longer hurt.
It's in you.
The bright to my smile
The company of a rainy night
My pillow I lay on
Timeless love that follows us behind.
Baby I've found in you.

What in earth did that mean?! So I carried on in my destructive ways. Even attempted to keep my style I once had in Jersey by thieving my clothing, accessories and better for the word any damn thing I wanted...I had skills. I was my mother's child. Well it came to a halt when one day I had to baby-sit my younger sister Reesy, "the snitch".

Coming out of Zayre's across the bridge from Riverview Terrace. I had loaded the baby carriage up with all the accessories, colors, and perks of a complete wardrobe. My m.o. was to baby-sit a child and subject their innocence to such behavior of shoplifting. I have gotten away with it enough where I felt comfortable. Then as it always does the day had come. This time Reesy accompanied me and as I ran after being called out she stay behind refusing to run and squealed like a pig.

It was my first trip to the detention center after being caught. Taken away as the thief I was, as it was inherited from the generational curse of my mother. I remember, lonely nights in a cold and dark room. Allowed only what they, "the (authorities)" was to give you. T.V. time, light meals, and outside yard time on specific time slots. I felt so alone that flirtation became my friend. Flirting with other misfits was my first start of picking the wrong boys for all the wrong reasons.

Those wrong reasons helped to build the character that makes you, or break you. My aspect of life at this time as I just recently learn is to love yourself before you can love anyone else. The low self esteem a majority of people mistakes on how cute or pretty someone thinks they are. All in another part of that is to love who is inside.

The person that makes you smile, cry or just feel a special feeling. Hug yourself with the warm words of wisdom, courage and strength. Kiss yourself with the softness, gentle, and of finesse to be who you want to be, and know that to be that person isn't a single move but a collage of inspiring works of arts that you obtain in you.

Since I didn't learn this at that moment, I got married to the first one that told me he love me as a repeat from how I loved him.[1] Marriage, let's see to hold, cherish, and protect…. something along those lines. What in hell did I know about marriage? I had already become intimate since 13 my husband is my third; I'm his first so I guess we start by teaching each other what the other doesn't know.

He knew nothing of loving himself coming from a broken home and loving me meant to control me. Control what I did, how I speak, when I think and all else was to come from his young childish ways of what he learned a man's position was. To me the marriage meant a better way of life and someone to share it with.

Still in High school, I went through the uhhh of all the stares of being his wife. As he sent me back and forth home to my mother as he had his wildest dreams filled to be the player he had become. I took the greyhound down the waters of Florida to the cold of Ohio so I may be what and who he needed me to be.

---

[1] STEVE HARVEY – 2/10/09 WBLS HITTING A WOMAN (INNER ABUSE)

A Queen Unheard

She has a voice. ...strong loud but unheard
When you doubted and had disbelieved..it was her
It was her strength when you were weak,
Her embrace to build back the peace
Her intentions, her quality of a human being.
It's She.
The backbone of reality. .the one who hurts more of what it brings. It is I.
A Queen unheard unrecognized.
It's my eyes closed tight, praying at the crack of dawn for Us all,
For You and I.
My Walk my calf my leg who strides the furthest
And furthermore stands only in your corner

It is Me..it is she
Elsewhere as well feeling my shoes
That another man chooses not to hear
Consider or understand.
Her. It is our wombs that bring life
How dare you categorize me as to neglect how to
Properly take care of One?
A Queen unheard, in a sense of hurt
But to be anything other than Her
To me is absurd. .because this Queen
Was chosen...to birth this universe
I am Hher.
A Queen, unheard.

It was very comfortable upon arriving with his family. His uncle and aunt were a loving couple who loved their kids dearly. It was a mirror of what a family should be, treated with respect and love. I began feeling like they were my family and to this day I will always have love for them. The wife (Aunt Ritha) was loving, pretty, energetic and a homemaker out of this world. The Husband (Uncle Fred) was always out making odd and ins out of life to bring home a dollar and feed the family. They didn't have much but they made it feel plentiful of love and care.

I feel most families should have this experience at one time or another to get the feeling of what it is all about "Family". Everyone have there flaws, but they kept their quarrels quiet and to a minimum and their discipline was strong valued with firm beliefs of right from wrong. A value that is instilled from a child, that some just miss the definition on how to apply it and abide by it. Right from wrong is something that should be considered first in every decision we make, it helps us to decipher what is important in life.

I concentrated on not being the bum my grandfather always called my mother, as an inspiration for me to become a better person. I graduated top 15 in my class and made the finish line. I skipped the prom, class trip and all that teenagers cherish for many years to come. I stayed on my game to be the best supporting wife I could. That meant to forget who I was to become.

Who would that be? Can I become the writer I wanted to be years ago? Could I become the poet, as I loved to speak? A motivational speaker since I led many with advice that I can direct but not follow? All that I dreamed was to be underneath him the man that made me feel I was a part of something. That is terribly pathetic! A man shouldn't make you feel nothing that you can't by yourself.

The marriage was what you would call convenient, for me it was a way to be grown and for him it was away from his home. We lived in our own, paid bills and worked together to keep it all in tact. Unfortunately, the cheating drove me crazy; he was to confess to confuse me into thinking that made it better. I forgave, even talked to the women to answer my questions hoping to ease the pain. It helped me to get to the trust issues I have now.

And to think all of that was before bearing my first child at 19 years old. After all of it, I should have run the other way. Instead, I insisted on concentrating to graduate high school and ignore the nudging issues. I moved back with my husband during my pregnancy to my hometown, where I felt safe.

Arriving in NJ, I started at "Seymour Wilson's (Poppy)" home. He was my grandfather, but I give him a full name title because of his temperament. He was strong, stern, and little to no tolerance for anything else other than what he would accept. He said I would grow to be a bum since I got married, so I figured he would have hated my new husband that he had met for the first time. Quite the contrary though, it was as if he was the grandchild rather than me.

It winded up being that they had more in common than just me. I would find myself covered in green sometimes against that man that took me through more drama than ever, and the man who did not trust anything of my being. It was a challenging time as a pregnant woman, for me my emotions were everywhere. At this time though I saw the most sensitive time with "Poppy", he was considerate of my morning sickness, easy with the roads while driving, and even worried of my health when it didn't appear I was dressed for the weather.

I had taken a part-time job with "Poppy" as his school bus aide. Lamar (my husband) had started working as a forklift driver in town. We worked hard and saved to get out on our own and by the time the baby was born we were. She was beautiful; I thought she was the answer to a finally faithful husband….notttt! He left me home alone more, stay out late even more than that and my greatest hint was when his friends took it upon their self to flirt with me behind his back.

I finally got back into the work field as a Bank Teller. It was great; a start of a career and the boredom went away. As I started feeling more confident the eyes followed me. Stares, flirtation, and even offers, at first I was leery of accepting than I said why the hell not, he hadn't any hesitation on what he did! Let the games begin?!

So we spent the first 4 years close in town by my grandparents home, until one day my game got cut short to say the least. His name was Isaac, and he had an effect on me. He happened to know one of the other tellers and got my name out the phone book. On one of my days off he called and surprised me not only by the call but the persistence of getting my number. I was still quite young 19 and he was a little younger 17 years of age. Very mature for his age and a picture to look at, if you know what I mean.

It was many nights of my husband out playing ball late and I had visits while the baby was sleeping. I used to even sneak out to serve him the dish I cooked for the day to show the little things that I loved to do. The sex was great and very attentive to my essential needs. He answered all of my calls and would be where I needed him to be at the drop of my dime. The question is after about 6 months I wondered why is it he was always at his uncle's house and not at home, so I rung the doorbell.

To my surprise it wasn't his uncle but the girl he had pregnant uncle's home. So as his bubble got busted that afternoon, mine got busted by evening. He had to prove his non involvement with me by telling where I lived to be approached by his girl!

As I stepped out my car with my groceries, my husband grabs me by the arm and pulls me to the front door of our apartment. As I fussed and cussed as to what the hell was his problem, I came face to face with my mouth being dropped with his special other. He stayed to the fact it was me who did the chasing and he wasn't interested. That was the beginning of a new chaos for me.

After this known betrayal, things weren't the same. I escaped down to Florida with my mother in hope that I can find a new beginning by myself with my daughter. I took the greyhound bus all the way, where there was a lot of thinking that took place. When I got there, it wasn't at all what I expected. Rumors flying everywhere against my mother that offended me terribly.

I thought when she had moved it was for the better, no more drug use and a change for her, unfortunately my little sister saw more than I did since I was off with marriage. She went from one addiction to another alcohol started to take over her life. First it started as socialization, as she worked as a Housekeeper. All her friends found her to be amazingly funny.

After just a few days of feeling that this wasn't the life I wanted for me and my daughter, a surprise came my way. Once again my husband returned for mercy all the way from New Jersey. He took the time to sweep me off my feet and convince me there will be once again change. We took the greyhound back together and talked the whole time on what we needed, wanted and what was to change in our lives. He then asked me for a son, we didn't hesitate once we returned home to make that happen and I successfully got pregnant as planned.

We (Lamar and I) moved to the far suburbs away from all of my known area. At first it appeared to be fine, more communication and a little bit more time spent as a family and things done as HE wanted, in the meanwhile I was trapped without a phone, car, or any friends. Another way of his controlling ways that kept me thinking this is the way it supposed to be. As a young bride I was very naive, cook, clean and sex. It was then that meeting Teisha was the beginning of a new lesson.

Teisha was a close friend that just being neighbors and speaking made me comfortable. She was vibrant strong and polite. Living so far from everyone put an aspect on what was important, so I made new friends. She made me realize I was being mentally abused.

I visited with Teisha on several occasions our kids played together, we talked and befriended almost instantly. It became an outing to me to go over her home, have some wine a little dresses (weed), and just the feeling of being myself for a moment.

Feeling alone and all made my God work in mysterious ways. Lamar locked the doors to know when I left out of the home and even sometimes watched me from down the street when pretending to go to work. After an accident with Lamar at work, it changed our paths tremendously. We were forced to make changes and our goal was to own a home.

So out of the saddened drama we had to move to a different destiny. God has always been on time, he sent us on the way to the Peach state in honors of a new start for us and our children. With "GA on our mind" we set on a 3 month goal.

He moved ahead with relatives until I packed and moved boxes while coming up with the down payment of a 3 br 2 ba home fenced in with fireplace and a beautiful ½ acre to decorate. We were young so we did the best we could moved in with relatives took on two jobs and a hustle and the real work began.

I was proud of us but during change the devil is always busy trying to put up obstacles and steer you away from your destiny. So as he went ahead he was responsible for just getting a job because it was included for 2 months of rent to be paid in advance. As always the thing from keeping a man to stay focus is his head below!

Those of you who knows Atlanta knows that there is no public transportation in the major suburb areas. Yes that an excuse now for male whorish ways, "She gave me rides". LOL. On this new journey we started out with stalking! He had met his ride to work who followed him to work, put letters in the mailbox and not letting go of the fact he was married. He didn't tell her he was married until it was convenient. He had no choice but to tell the truth.

Deceitful Lies of Lust

Lies of lust, to do as he must.
Love hate while hurting Me.
The story of many of Us.
The excessive excuses, covered with
Love making and smooches.
Clever to not believe
Yet this deceitful lust of lies..we as woman choose.
Just a stage to find pain, we have never before gained.
And after said and done, more than often
We are positioned to pass on their name.
A name of shame.
But we didnt think of that lost in love.
How insane.
You tell me to love..I feel to do different. But in the moment,
    being naiive and down for you,
I am in this.

A chain still yet to be broken amongst us as Queens.
Deceitful lies of lust tolerated.
Rise Up, you are better than this..
Do Believe.

A scorned woman at work; I decided to fix Ms. Stalker, with a little taste of her own medicine. Dressed in my attire for, seeking a job look. Approached her place of employment and awaited the floor manager. As she was walking in I stuck my hand out for a soft shake. She was pointed out by the receptionist and I wore my smile of this is interest to you.

"There is an employer of yours that has been stalking my family since I moved to the area". Employers don't accept this behavior no matter what your seniority. After notification of the employee first and last name in addition to arranging my made flyers to notify co workers of a hotline- 1-800-FOR-SLUTS for such information on "Slut's behavior" (of course I used her real name!).

Now the begging starts, baby, please forgive me it was a mistake I would never do it again, (at least until I screw my customer of the business you help me start)! Yes his customers became his mistresses, once a man feel confident he can get away with something he runs it in the ground. I was slow at the game I had slickness about me from what I learned from Kita who taught me "guys are always a game" that's the only way to stay on top of it.

Well after going through all the "Whys, How's, and what's wrong with you stage, you move on with dignity. Walk the talk and talk the walk, as my uncle would say your bark is bigger than your bite he heard it all before in which you are wasting your time. I got my job, worked, saved, and tried to move on with him until the obvious was seen. Red light specials, favorite dinners, even porno……what ever strokes his ego! It was the way to show I cared but yet let him know what he would be missing once it's gone. A woman can only stand some what's of the abuse that causes insanity!

Would've, could've, should've all the things you replace his betrayal with placing the blame on yourself rather than what the real issues were. Their ego needs to be stroked 24/7 without you're bound to get the shaky grounds on which shatters or find new branches. Our new start was the branch instead he fell through the tracks and became broken from the relationship.

I got started on a real estate career and became content with being something other than a house wife. It felt lucrative and filling of my soul. I had my own income coming in and was still able to contribute towards the bills. Of course that became a problem, now I wasn't cooking balanced meals and I'm never home. The fears of infidelity on his behalf became my surrounding. I didn't let it bother me at first, but later it became the reason of his worst fear.

Someone that made me feel, special and attractive once again. He was just a city worker but he had a voice of a robin. He cooked and made the atmosphere relaxing, productive and always had a nice word to say. Yeah, I know they all do in the beginning and the grass always look greener on the other side. It was certainly a relief from the drama I had experienced!

When all the drama dies there is the pain and loneliness that has to be stretched to the reality of misery. It becomes a constant reminder that your dream of anything positive has been destroyed. Only the strong rises above because no one person has the right to have dominion of your mental health. Rising above means to claim what your destiny is directing your own path without the negative energy.

Love We Dreamed of

When he puts his lips on me, my body
Releases a quiver.
A mental note of pure gold.
Sold.
I am. To that man, with the greatest tongue.
Of all land, I shiver in pleasure.
Ive never felt so amazing letting
Down my hair.
For you to go there. Our lips now of pairs
Giving me all of what can be delivered,
How dare.
I be silent, the back of my eyelids
I stare.
In awe of your empowerment
To have astonishingly gone and
Over the top because of it.

I claimed my path by denying my husband any rights to my heart. I worked hard and played hard with no respect or regards to what was known as marriage. What was good for the goose was also good for the gander in my book. He liked to portray family knowing that behind doors it was just a mirror image. I accepted that concept it was less pain for me to feel and even more less to explain!

We lived three years in the home with this attitude just to say Divorce took place in 1997. I went to the store fed up and never returned home. Apartment home book in hand and skipped out on that month's mortgage. He's the man he had no conscious on what was going on so he did what he felt best for him and so did I.

We took a season in each other's lives and then it was done. I took away with me my ambition that I learned through Lamar insisting I went to business school and he prospered in his family business that was encouraged by our relationship. So that was our reason in God's name.

I took the next step to move on, and then life started in the single life. It started out glamorous. I had no one to answer too, no one to ask anything of me, and it was all about what me and my kids needed and making it happen. I taught strength and independence in the way only experience could. Eventually it came to meet someone who knew how to make me feel like someone important.

When becoming a woman you get things that are deserved when showing you are a woman of integrity and dignity. Nice places to go, things to see, enjoyment of nature, fine dining and all the things of your heart as a Queen desires. Treat yourself like the Queen you are and all else will follow, just have your heart in order strong enough for the snakes and games that are always thrown to you as curve balls.

I later found my son's father but before he became that he was a great influence in my life on what love should be. We were each other's shadow not by jealousy or force but by the want of making each other happy. It was at least 3 months before I found he abandoned his family and as the saying goes it will happen to you too.

Always know it is a third story of every relationship. It is his story, her story and the truth. I thought that the constant calls on his phone were regarding late payments of child support. We were actually at his job picnic with all who knew he had a family and was married all except me. He made me feel he knew to give me anything I want, appeared to be a prominent man of virtue. Took me to the park on one knee to request us starting a relationship…..how sweet right, yeah it would have been if he wasn't already married!

He cooked cleaned, home improvements and fixed cars…..the perfect all around man, I thought! I was very happy for months out of our 3 years of a relationship at least 10 months all the rest was supporting habits and cleaning up messes it started a trend in relationships with me based all around "Alcohol". That's why strong hearts with the knowledge to distinguish BS is necessary in a positive relationship.

Being sheltered in my marriage and living in the suburbs most of our lives, made me not see the destruction men can cause in people lives. The lies, deceit, the faces of devils with a smile! I have been going in circles for years trying to make a good man of what I accepted in my life as settling.

Well to complete the happy life with Keith my younger son's father it ended in an escapade of abandonment as was foreseen by his wife. He now tries the best he can to support financially which helps the situation but in my son's heart I'm sure he is now feeling the abandonment! The cycle goes on.

It was a challenge dealing with an angry 12 year old I left out of town with Keith for 6 months without my twin (my daughter). I missed an important day (9th grade graduation) of hers in which I will always regret but I became selfish when the marriage ended a part of me had disappeared. She was angry about the divorce, she was angry she had to live with her dad and now she had to make sacrifices since a man can't really raise a daughter without some woman's input, and believe me his virtues wasn't what should be remembered.

It was all a matter before she was forced to grow up in an environment she had not appreciated, one without her mother. Cherie (my daughter) had grew first to be angry, then to be responsible and forced into puberty with emotions being unable to place correctly with no knowledge on what was going on. Emotions that probably couldn't even be understood as a woman so intense. My props goes out to her with how well she handled all that came her way with the strength that she was taught without even knowing it was soon to be used.

Upon our return Keith and I, we took over my ex-husband's apartment and brought our family together. It was more resentment and fireworks from the previous (current) then "Mrs." She was determined not to let us be together happily. We thought that leaving the state would give her time to cool off.

Unfortunately, by time we returned chaos was worst since Keith didn't mention her family was under the impression he was to seek employment with the family business to regroup for their sake.

I definitely don't think his mistress (me) was a part of the plans but it was his deceit that kept it all separate to give him peace of mind for the short while in which I got pregnant once again. He had obviously later found been bouncing back in forth between the two of us spreading stories to keep each of us happy.

Deceit always bring you to another path, his brought him incarceration. Several charges were brought with threats over the phone to a Police officer a set up by the "Mrs." Just short of saying he missed our son's whole young life because he spent it behind bars. Before the final determination it was another moment of my heartbreak that was proven by his actions that he was to be with his wife when I was bringing our than 2 week old son to him and he gave our first abandonment lesson.

Then it was the abandonment of his arrest that left his son and I in the parking lot when he fled before that final determination, yet and still through it all he was angry at us for our abandonment and not serving 6years with him after finalizing his divorce from the inside. I never believed it was going to happen and once again moved on!

I think this was also the time I had to deal with an additional burden, my mother's death! My divorce wasn't even final yet in early December 96' my sister Reese says, "I don't think Mommy is going to make it through Easter", I never forget those cold words and how it made me feel. Of course, I brushed her off and said stop saying things like that. Amazingly at this time I had talked to my mother every day. You find that as an adult you can become friends before all the flaws in the relationship effects you.

My mother's death took place in 1997, I was only 28 and she was only 48 years of age. She was taken from us for her abuse of alcohol. It had made her liver weak and her color turned an ill grey. With all she didn't give to me, it was more of what I did get from her that hurts me the most. It's a funny thing but whoever our parents are and what lives they lived with us we must know we only have one mother and one father, if we had even been blessed to know them.

They say things happen in threes, I can vouch for that from bad to worst in a moment of a finger snap.

After struggling through that abandonment as his wife once did between maintaining life for the children and keeping sanity literally. I fell into a financial crush and was forced to move in with my sister. I was determined not to stay long to inconvenience her life no more than I had too. I worked two jobs and met someone to care for our then 9 month old son. I worked during the day and night to save money first for a vehicle, then for a down payment into our own apartment. It took 8 months, I'm proud to say.

I wind up after all those events packing it up and forced out of town due to financial hardship and moved in with my sister. She has always been a blessing to me. As children we weren't raised together and our sisterhood wasn't bonded until later. I became a part of her life when God sent me to be. I take this moment to say I love my sister dearly and hope she knows that she will always be a part of me.

She has accomplished so much in her life from such a hard road she had to follow, it was her strength, determination and good heart that led her to prosperity. She had always had a soft spot for children and taking care of them, I feel her blessings her just rising from it all and her destiny was to be a messenger of God, I promise to tell her story after this book is published and successfully distributed in Jesus name I claim!

On this journey to regain all that I had lost before my move in, I was again determined not to have my children live less than what they deserve. My children at this time, was still living with their father during the transition. I began to work almost immediately, the one thing I would always be grateful of Lamar (my ex-husband) is the Business School he inspired me to go to since I was so anxious to satisfy my grandfather wishes.

The trade I learned there was for my typing, computer and Accounting skills that I use even today, it has never left me without the opportunity to have a job. My office job was my savings and my second job as a server is what we lived off of until I reached my goal.

Once I was settled my daughter returned with me and my son decided he wanted to stay and help his father with his business. Here it was a baby and a teen, worked out well to continuously afford the lifestyle I wished for them. We lived across from the golf course with all the amenities. How much of it really was used probably just the screened in patio porch where I did most of my entertaining. It was available for whenever we wanted to explore our options.

School systems was always a plus that I wanted to be sure that my daughter had an opportunity to strive and be her best. Of course though as usual Cherie had her own ideas of what she wanted. She got bored with our lifestyle, no drama or action taking place. Too much, safety and hope, go figure. As teens, they are always curious of what they can't see or experience. Cherie took that to a whole new level.

My children are my hearts and they are all their individual strong spirited, souls. That daughter (my one and only) of mine taught me some new stuff! She is the wild spirit that I earned to be but didn't have in me to take it that far. She went places, I wouldn't dare so young, did things I only thought of and was confident that whatever she did was the way it should be done. Never, was a dull moment with Cherie.

If I had a moment to take a ride in her mind I think it would be a roller coaster ride. She reminded me so much of my little sister Reese, I felt she was more of her child in her younger days then mine. Daring, exciting, witty, and street savvy. Something I had always seemed to lack, I never was informed enough on what the streets could teach. Common sense can be learned from travels of the hood and the way of living on the streets. This may not seem something that you need; I'm here to tell you it is!

There are a lot of Degree received graduates that can't find their way out of a wet paper bag. The reason being common sense is needed as a life skill that may be used in the most detrimental moment. When common sense is lacked your vulnerable to all those that do have it and can use it against you. I had first- hand experience with the personal relationships that were able to get me in unnecessary fact finding situations and lead to most of my criminal activities of mischief and domestic violence.

Drunken Love Misunderstood

Infatuated with your sweet nothings
In my ear of a drunken mind...
Sounds beautiful though.
I smile at every lie.
In lust not love.
Was just you and I
...I was the sheep yet leading us both blind
I dazed in the thought imagining
You were for me and I can make you change.
One drink led only to another
A roller-coaster of pain.
How selfish to think to be in love
And then bare you a child of your name

Knowingly you have not or ever will be
The image I want of my child to be framed..
Life though huh. Teaches you the ropes
And to stay in your lane
Know who you lay up with, before playing this game

One thing I can say I had successfully finished all requirements to complete my criminal correction activities, but it still effects my life now although it was so long ago. This is why I let everyone know when you know you have a temperament that can lead you in a path that may go longer then you are willing to travel, choose your battles carefully! Everyone whether upon admissions or not has a battle in themselves that can simply lead to destruction but there are those that has been choosing their battles and not taking the chance on consequences that they're not ready for.

Consequences, is a very strong word. It is not to be taken lightly, especially if you have motherly tendencies to protect your seed no matter what! That may be worthy of any consequence. However, the typical man isn't! Trouble over nonsense that could have been prevented because of jealousy, misguidance or deceit hasn't been able to be understood by society.

It's a fine line between love and hate is what comes to mind to describe the anger that is felt during a betrayal of trust. Going back to my incidents it was one moment of feeling so loved, admired and cherished to feeling the bottom of a shoe for all the disrespect thrown by actions of a typical man action of ludicrously. Ludicrous is the word I use because knowing me as a person you should know I do not take rejection nor disrespect lightly!

My feelings have been mixed and confused for a while now so I decided to start this journal. I have four children and 3 grandchildren. I feel by the time the grandchildren are old enough to know what life is I want them to believe and know life is what you make it. Something I still grow into it since in my life my heart feels overwhelmed in loving a man who seems to hate me. Oh no, he doesn't say that he always says he loves me yet he makes strong statements in his beliefs that lines up against me.

I try keeping him company and talk with him I'm talking to much I show that I would appreciate his time he runs like hell in the midst of a court date that we have created its like he's just keeping peace until its over and then we are.

So I'm to be realistic in knowing this but instead I try hard to show him I love him and my past decisions has effected us but I'm willing to stand strong through it all. His attitude is he doesn't live with me so there fore no commitment nor any suggestion of it my heart breaks every day since I know he doesn't truly love me.

Let's see today starts with the thoughts in my mind after S.C. 7/23 weekend returning to the facts of a full relationship he had since 5/5/09 with another. They had all the opportunity to disclose the truth but she was blinded by his lies the same as I was. The only thing is she knew he spent his time with me as a couple and I thought she was something to start not realizing it was well on its way started off the grounds in despicable actions against me and all that I felt for him.

Continuously we go back n forth on how he kept the truth from me. He says it was my fault for the rejection he felt while incarcerated. So now its denial of his actions I'm supposed to accept it all and swallow in dumb founded blinded love for him. Let's see I was strong willed from the beginning of this relationship I felt he can offer what I needed with just a push.

Now 3 years later he reflects all I did was ruin him and I expect too much of him he cant deliver. So out of anger I lash out during pregnancy with his son after his promise of rehab and making it better so I will conceive and deliver his first live born son. After disappointment I'm even angrier and lash out more at his binges of horrible words and disrespect to our financial plan.

After being raged at me for not continuing to put up with it all he reacts against me to attack and his actions finds him incarcerated. I wasn't the role model of the jail house rock that faulted me for more disrespect and started the affair with so much anger against me but yet never could let me go since no one else was to have me. I find out through the months of him going back and forth as a player he portrayed.

She was introduced to family and kids all a while I was in the dark about the betrayal against me. I took much time to sill dedicate a purpose of our relationship. Find him a career escalate his funds even portray a family with our boys. He hated me and loved me the same day loved her too here with me as a convenience since usury is his middle name. Now he expects me to accept calls to another woman conversation as a backup to our problems I call her his clean up woman. His ego is based on his flips, dancing, and the ability to keep up with the young bucks.

Another day awakening to fear disappointment and disgust. Last Saturday my son's father took my baby and car to his ex-girlfriend's house, a girlfriend that was kept in a secret affair for 3 months behind my back and started right in front of my face at his family function, all in of course his intoxication. I tried to put him out respecting we don't need anymore trouble with the law so I abandoned him at his mother's in hop of ending all this pain and anxiety of what is my problem to accept this nonsense.

I was told to evaluate why I needed him back into my life besides the hope of every woman's dream to be a family. He's the most loving man without alcohol for the moment but at my age now I want to travel, purchase finer things be able to primp myself up every other week without worrying what bill won't be paid all things you do when you have support but I can't do any of those things.

Being patience, is the virtue but with the alcohol. There is no sanity to our relationship everything just becomes my fault in his eyes. I have to hear constantly about his ex wife I know her complete description of her body, her thoughts, and I was even told she is the best woman he knows. I know her personal life style through him. I should accept all this because he has daughters with her..... What the hell!!!!

Absolutely not! It is not acceptable because I'm special and deserve so much more, his lost if he doesn't know that! I think a couple more fights and threats of my freedom brought me to the reality it is over! I can't dwindle under his shadow taking away from my well being just because I feel he needs someone. Ladies, understand there is no raising of a grown man that is done by mothers not ladies of their lives. As someone once told me there is no excuse for a man he is to make it happen....on that note he is to ride out on his own.

I have accepted that after many chances to prove himself he hasn't even begun to accept change is needed. I love him enough to let him go. If we can't prosper together than we are no good for each other. At least that is my philosophy, unfortunately he had a little bit trouble accepting that. He has a strong family intuition that the mother of his child should always be his. That is a great thought, but it also takes work to make it happen.

Work to build a relationship, work to stay in a relationship and work to keep important things in mind. It is hard to do any of that if manhood isn't instilled. He was spoiled first from his maternal grandmother then with his wife, both gave him the agenda that it wasn't a man's job to provide. It was easy for him to get finance without working nor earning it. When it comes easy there is no hardship or acceptance to what shall be in place.

Manhood is a learned behavior. It must be instilled and grounded in our boys. As a mother of three boys, it starts from early on. It isn't good to spoil our boys or is it valuable to let things go without sweat! Earn a living, save your money, treat with respect and respect your elders. This is the main circumstances a boy needs to become a, there is no excuse for a man and he is the provider no matter what!

If you need a man to do what he must do know his relationship with his mother. Mothers are dear with our boys and if she doesn't accept his behavior, actions, or current status most likely he has not been in coordinate of his actions as a man. I only wish I knew that before falling in love and adding a child that again have to go without a strong, ready financially, emotionally nor to become a mentor.

I am stepping out of my boundaries and into a new circle of all positive rewards! I know there are some things for me to work on me, but I demand that time for myself and will extend my every being on being successful of my life! My personal goals will be separated from my professional goals and I will make that Diva out of me if it's the last thing I do!

Where do I start, emotionally....what makes me happy! I want to be a family right now it doesn't include a man to be onsite, but someone in my life with character of strength, motivation and a clear path on where he is going, no more lost souls.

How do I make that family happen by completing myself emotionally knowing all the things I want in a gentleman of my life to be upcoming or completed in my own? My finances shall be in place to take up the dreams I have to travel – long term. Short term, is to change my daily habits of health, happiness and devotion to me. I demand to better developed of my goals and using my time to get there.

I will do less sleeping more action, not just the typical household duties but to step to mind theory actions. I think I need motivation then I will get to my music to relax my mind and put it in motion. I think I need to create hobbies I will take my funds and process what I want to do. What is it all "Action required!"

I'm a professional first; I try to think professional at all that I do. What does most professionals do become entrepreneur and open businesses? I need to be able to hold something dear that will require my attention and complete with the idea I can pass to my children or grandchildren for them to cherish. I can no longer use any excuse my time is running and I'm getting no younger I must reach a success at this point in my life!

It should always be considered of your health habits as well, I feel my bones aching, more body fat than ever, and the energy level of a 90 year old woman. I must increase my mental state next which follows from good healthy habits to form the condition you need to be in to reach your highest standards.

Something I instill in my "Fabulous Four" (my children), is to be strong, independent, reliable and respectful first and the Lord will see you through! I have my Daughter who through her rebellious stages came out like a champion. She is a wonderful mother who teaches pretty much the same tactics – especially "Independence and Respect"! She goes within her means to be responsible, resourceful and unpredictable with my babies (grands), and for that I'm proud of my "Baby girl".

As for my babies I have my upcoming super star "Butterball" that I foresee, don't know exactly what but he is going to be the best at it and make the money, honey. My little precious "Diva" isn't going to be taking no slack off of anyone; she is showing early she is not with the game!

My son, Donavan has stepped up to be a wonderful father, soldier, and a man of virtue! He is my proud "Marine" and thanks me every chance for my attitude of not being a little "Bi-atch" in life. I can say since his graduation of high school he has learned more about manhood within these last 3 years than the average grown man who can't hold a candle. Knowing the life of woman through his sister and I, he is sure to see his son as often as his career allows him to my "Little Man".

Then there is Stephon my younger son still at home who appears to have the looks of his older brother and personality (attitude) of his big sister. I always teased her since I was always busy working and she held the household down that it was those moments that he grew to be just like her. He is laid back, calm, and mischievous but yet respectful as well very loving. I can always depend on a hug and a smart mouth to make me laugh and this is why he will always move my heart.

Also, the baby of the family that I failed to mention is the same age as my grands. He is a character on his own by a long shot! He likes to flirt with those big round eyes of his and already frisky with his hands, I feel he will be the brain of the operation. He stands small but he's always thinking fast and moving quick on his feet. "Houdini" his nickname of course is always on the move and showing that little mind of his is on a mission!

My "Fabulous Four" has been a part of my journey and an inspirational guide of making it all come together. I want them all to know never to give up on your dreams and to always strive higher than what you know you can achieve. Life is lived by our character, dreams and hopes in which all should be touched every day of our lives. We are to make most of the small things that will make us laugh, and hold dear those who are important in order to live big in our days.

In all of my life I have learned lessons late, and been chasing my tail for years. This journal is to encourage those to extend their expectations, expand their dreams and to live to the upmost of what is capable of you. Sometimes, we have to reach further than the stars to feel the outcome of life we like to live. If you don't expect anything of yourself than nothing will become of you and regrets will follow with you and any of your extended family.

Remember our lives usually are mimicked by someone in our lives. They see your weaknesses, strengths and ability way before you do because we are stumped by growth within ourselves. Recognize it, understand it and move from anything that stops you from being a meaning in life. Life is dictated by us in many ways, whether our power of words, decisions not to recognize the battles to choose, or the chances to take by just a thought of empowerment. Don't hestitate to step out on the limb as long as you know the branch is strong!

A Yearning for A Mother

Instead of the lead put into her arms, I wish it were me
Instead of the streets she strolled at night
I longed for a kiss Goodnight, or to be told
Sweetdreams
To pray together in thankfulness and hope
That everything will be alright
I needed her.. didn't she feel that
For the moments she was behind bars
Being a mother she didn't lack.
I craved the boys & bees lesson between us that never happened

Instead I married a fool
Believing in the moon and stars
A betrayed caption
With her young eyes to tattle and her being
There to imitate
What you should have taught me right from wrong
Give or take..
A hell of a difference I know this life would be
With my mother a love she didn't know how to feed
But it's her wity and determination
That even thru her wrongs I've distilled
To be the best at what I do, yes
A phenomenal Woman

Shadow of a Mirror

A drama of a mother raising a daughter in a distance of understanding and communication. Mother finds herself being a victim of friendship with her daughter. A friendship to be ceased abruptly. When puberty comes about the family has already reached divorce and separation of siblings. It is a struggle to be overcome yet a determination to be successful at the relationship to be of progress and hope. The findings are surprising and heartfelt.

Shadow of a Mirror

Cherie was my first born 2 days after her grandmother's birthday. She was conceived in Springfield, OH. It was a town of poverty and distress. I had just been through my husband's infidelity that made him send me home to my mother while he acted in his inappropriate ways. I wasn't sure what was going on at first, naïve to the facts. My husband stated he wasn't able to be a good provider and needed me to be home with my mother until he got it all together.

Little did I know that just meant, I'm tired of you and found someone new. I had served my purpose to get him away from his abusive family whom he lived with his parents in a Jehovah Witness environment. It was an excuse for their poverty and mishaps not to abide to their children's happiness. His mother was working on her second marriage and had a personal vendetta against Lamar for his being.

His circumstances made his childhood; his manhood was effected by not knowing what real love was. My real love was genuine until his misconceptions that forced me to look for that same genuine love elsewhere. Two wrongs don't make a right, but in my world what was good for the goose was good for the gander! Unlike Lamar, I knew my sexiness and my affect on the male companions. I received what I needed for the time I wanted it.

I need to say there is a bigger consequence from female ganders than male gooses, at the least pregnancy --- which is responsible for the being to be cared for. In a marriage it is your husband! Unfortunately, it isn't fair to bring in a life unless you are fully responsible yourself. No one can know what the other will do; you are only responsible for your own actions.

I also can say that with the "Jezebel Spirit" I inherited it was more than my actions I had to monitor. It's something about the way I sway when I walk (completely natural), my hazel eyes and my confident persona. It has always giving me more attention than I can handle. I always knew how to handle myself well within my standards of being well beyond grown at 15.

It appeared after stating a little background on Cherie's parents that I return to how she became so witty, curious, street smart, sensitive and ghetto in such a form that she just got bored with the typical living. As a small child she always liked attention and loved to smile and pose for the camera. I remember at 6 months she was well aware on how to get what she wanted or knew how to get it. She would be alert to her surroundings in knew when to sneak around to retrieve what she knew was not to be touched.

It was as if temptation was her weakness. She was tempted by childhood to turn into a game from school. She didn't enjoy exploring what she didn't have she wanted to touch what she did have. I guess her temptations were growing even back then. She did everything early potty training, posing with confidence, smooth her way out of Daddy's trenches and most of all she became diva of getting attention! I think she was four when we moved to Ga.

When we (parents) were going through infidelities she was the first to notice. Didn't know what she was acknowledging but for sure it wasn't right. "Mommy", she stated, some woman is walking in our driveway. "Ma, why daddy always going to do that lady's yard and don't be outside?" She would even be the one to notice my clothes, accessories and my daily tasks. I think through all of this she was growing fast and thrown in with realities without even realizing it.

As woman we get our strength very early in life. Remembering back to my child hood I had to be forced to be independent and aware of what my family needs was. My older sister endured cooking meals that weren't provided at age 8. She was to make bread and peanut butter last through six children. Then worry if her mother was to even come home to provide the next meal. There was no room for concern for her personal growing needs.

When mother did show up she was usually doped up on heroin or passing out with the after effects of the drugs used. Money wasn't an issue with or without it the younger children had to be fed, whether that meant the older ones don't eat or not. It was mind boggling how we all got through it, but I definitely know it wasn't an option! The strength comes from inner soul with the grace of God looking out for the babies and the fools.

A mother daughter relationship is hard to come by when true, blue and filled with joy. I always know you only have one mother no matter what! The relationship is what needs to be circumstances of the generations to come. A mother to tell your secrets to and know it will stay in between the two, or as I am in between my true friends. Cherie always hated me to share, but I know it went nowhere else because I selected my companions of life!

Sometimes sharing one's story may destruct another's relationship. The functioning between the two is that love is there. To share and gossip is one but to share and confirm or recollect on a prior experience is another possibility. We love to know there is someone going through what we went through. I think sharing the stories will make it better to endure the outcome.

We like to hide behind our true endeavors because it most of the time take us away from our character. Our character builds us and our history may be what breaks us. The true character takes what brings us down and learn how not to step with that walk again. Walking some paths can be hurtful, ugly and even destructive as a memory.

Some of my painful memories still are walking with me because I never learned to let go! The betrayals hurt so bad that you grit your teeth and bear the thought. I want this memoir to be about the relationship between a daughter and a mother. As woman we grow but the child stays within, therefore this will be my way of letting go. One of the times I endured pain I couldn't believe was happening is where I will start.

I was about 14 and I left my home because I loved (love???) my boyfriend, I up and left what I had to nothing. Roam the streets and go from house to house to find comfort, just to be with him. Homeless and on the run, but yet I went to school every day. It was the way to keep focus.

He promised me marriage and he kept his promise. It was the betrayal of after giving up so easily what I had for him and moving away as a married couple that all he had to repay me was not even six months to move on.

I took a long trip on the greyhound bus after telling him I missed him so and needed to be with him. He moved from our apartment to his grandmother's and during the move it was a companion he shared it all with. I received pictures from him right before my trip that "showed off his muscularity" at least that was what the woman's handwriting said on the back of the picture.

I had ask him to explain who the woman's writing was, he simply said someone who did his hair. I took that picture all over the world looking like a complete fool before actually asking. That was my first hint. The second hint was his family members asking what was our relationship status. "What do you mean, I love my husband". Well obviously he had shown otherwise to his family by parading his new squeeze.

I was still unaware of the facts though. It was one of his confessions that let it all be known. He had this thing if he confesses it clears him of guilt. He says, "I met her at work, we were just friends". So the first thought is so now what? She was smart enough not to give up anything; she was in college and went on her merry way after breaking his heart.

Where did that leave me watching him call her, cry over her, and trying to ignore the truth? Although, the truth to me was, what was I missing that he couldn't love me that way? I know her name to this day, never ate at the restaurant they met at, and cringe every time I thought of her destroying what was supposed to be my marriage.

Yes, I blamed her! I was once told you can run quicker with your skirt up than your pants down. You never know what she was told though, men lie, lie, and lie! Lying is to protect them, or just to get what they want. I'm just recognizing that now though, how funny life gets when you get a clearer picture. If that wasn't enough to humiliate me and turn me ill towards him, take this……!

At this time I'm in my senior year of high school, Married and all about "MY HUSBAND". I had given up prom, senior class trip and was on welfare to make sure we can survive on our own. It wasn't even enough that I gave all that up, by now I know he just married me because he felt I was strong enough for him to get on with his life from his distraught childhood. He took this selfishness to talk me out of even thinking about leaving him. He had his joy while I was away and trying to heal his broken heart. The best way men know to heal is with another woman.

So his summer of heartbreak was the many women he dated that I had to eventually wind up in school with and listening to the whispers behind my back. My thoughts were, "What were they saying, thinking or even judging me as". The stares were treacherous, the disrespect was countless and as for me holding my temper was accounted for since nothing was directed at me! The anger at him was misplaced elsewhere trying to keep my marriage strong ….then I was passive, lol! I had to first deal with the fact my mother was sick and didn't have long.

The death of my mother gave me the power of soul searching since, it was a surprise but yet expected by her way of life. She went from drugs to booze and her lifestyle wasn't life it was death to come. Upon her passing, she was totally disrespected by her then boyfriend of 10 years. He allowed his new woman to cook the collards and clean their (my mother and his) kitchen. My sister heard the rumors but didn't suspect it could have been true, but was determined to find out.

It was an early morning call I received, I never forget it was a Saturday. My younger sister says, I have a key to the house and tonight I intend on using it to see if the rumors all over town were real. My immediate response was I'm on my way. Then reality was he (my mother's boyfriend) abused her and was Army background. My thought was to protect my sister and take the situation in control, then I bought a handgun.

I had a full paycheck a weapon I didn't know how to use, a friend taught me how to shoot and I was off to South Carolina from Virginia. I was driving 95 miles a hour and nervous. I got there 8 hours later and ran right into the drama. My sister was on the inside screaming and yelling on the demand to know who the woman was. When she approached me they immediate locked the door knowing my presence.

I took matters in my hand banging the doors and expecting someone to give me the little tramp whom disrespected my mother, who wasn't even in the ground yet! I was so angry and hurt the windows were next as I bang them out of the house I was thinking no one will have peace here! That led to the gun firing in the air to warn them it would be critical if she doesn't come out to face me now! My sister was out of control with fright and displacement.

This was an evening that affected the rest of our lives. It was a very emotional moment as well as discouraged for anyone to have been through what we did that evening. The officers called to the scene were not at all concern with the emotions nor the events that led to that moment. Their job is to deliver an arrest and be sure that it was beneficial to the count of records for their badge! I have learned since you pick your own battles and you are not to take it all in without thought and acting on emotions.

God handles those who aren't in seed of his word. In the meanwhile I had to pick up the pieces of my life and continue on with the distress of that evening affecting my life and bury the thoughts that haunted me while laying my mother to rest. She had a service of respect and love. We still had to deal with the bum that stepped all over her memory! After all was said, the couple remained together and much deserved each other. They are both terribly unhappy and stuck by marriage.

I had to get back to the beginning of the end of my marriage. I had consequences of my actions then and had to evolve my life around it while trying to live a normal life. It was hard since people see as a criminal when things end in an arrest. The charges were my first I had no idea what they meant or how it will be a deciding factor of life decisions, employment, reputation, and embarrassment.

It is however currently a reason to be involved in something meaningful for others that may have been in the same situation. Not keeping a cool head and a warm heart. It inspires actions of empathy, a bigger outlook on issues you would never find yourself thinking about. That one moment of distress caused a lifetime of pain and regret. Now I can think about the prisons filled with people of mistakes and confusion on why they can't have a second chance. Or those who get second chances and don't know how to go about change in their lives.

Let's see another time of complete soul destruction. After my divorce, I needed to be independent but yet feel some type of connection with the likes of being attached. So I met my middle son's father. He never mentioned he was married. What would I know? He took me to the family picnic at his job. He took me for a spending spree and even got on one knee to ask me to be his woman, how romantic! It was all a part of his Casanova style of getting the woman. I was so naïve coming from my sheltered marriage.

He even spent nights with me continuously, always was in place, I knew where his job was and even got paid when he did. The neighborhood knew us as a couple. I believed his love for me. How did I find out he was married? He so happen to leave his phone at my house when on his way to visit his kids. The shock had to be overwhelming when I answered the phone to speak with his daughter. So innocent "May I speak with my Daddy?

It was the next call that shocked me, "Where is my husband?"" Excuse me", I replied. He told me you would call with drama, since he missed your child support payments. She proclaimed, "I don't know what he told you but, he is currently my husband. We've been going through it the last 4 months and he moved out about 3 months ago. I think I was so distressed by this new perfect man in my life! It all came tumbling down, he convinced me he was unhappy for years and didn't want to lose what he felt was a good thing.

Where did I go from there? Destruction, he wanted his cake and eat it to continuously went back and forth (of course not with my knowledge at this time) threatening her, abusing the fact that he was busted and wasn't going to accept her with no one else. He called one night with his usual drunken drama and the police was there and heard his "Terroristic Threats". It was the night before the real drama came about when he went to the house to damage her male companion's car.

In the midst of all this sneaking and being unaware of all that was keeping me in the dark, I was being evicted. Heartfelt as I am helped me to decide to take my rent money to bail him out of jail. After all he was so giving with his funds for the now 8 months we were together. I gave my children to their father, and had to start all over. I had weekend visitations, and was close for them if they needed me. I resided in a hotel.

It felt so free, room service, no immediate responsibilities besides that weekly rent. I worked, he worked, and we took our time with all that we wanted too. We lived our lives like normal. Except it was nothing normal about all of this. I wind up having to take him to get his son, in which what time the still "Mrs." tried to commit suicide. She was rushed to a mental institution, where she thanked me for bringing her family.

If that drama wasn't enough we were still dealing with the arrest that was previously made and it consequences. This was the time that I visited back n forth and saw his Ex as well with baby in hand. All a while, she was contemplating getting her husband back by any means necessary. The lies he had to tell, and the promises she was making. A conspiracy, in which will lead up to my heartbreak.

The day of his release after 3 months, I waited in the lobby for him to come out. The shock was so was the wife. I had my baby then to be a few weeks old, He held him. She snatched his arm to direct him towards her. I'm standing wondering what is going on. He walking with the both of us as she tugged him and he's explaining that he's going home with her. I was totally confused that wasn't what our visits insisted of and his eyes were speaking different from what his mouth was.

I went home feeling betrayed, hurt but felt I needed to suck it up and drag my tail between my legs. After all it was her husband! I had just walked in the door after thinking all kind of thoughts, while driving. The room looked dark, and I fell to my knees in complete augh! My roommate ran to me as I screamed and she held me until I felt whole again. After a day of crying and hearing nothing from him he showed up at the door.

He had his kids with him and she was in the car, he was there to receive his clothes. Then later I get a call to pick him up far away on the other side of town at a hotel room. He said he had to go along with her because she held his future/freedom in her hands. He needed to get his toolbox from her house to work with and finish business before he could return to me. That was the story he told me but what was the story he told her??

She called me and stated they will be finalizing their marriage to be renewed tonight. He was to stay away until she was able to talk to the older kids of his return. Well why was he calling me, better yet why did I respond. Looking for love in all the wrong ways and places the story of my life. You don't have to work so hard and go through so much if it is right.

Again, that wasn't a thought then just another lesson learned later in life. The turmoil was to be over when he returned with me and faced the music of his consequences betraying her once again. She even called and said she foreseen him in prison for 10 years. He was so confused on what should have been of his life but he did know he was unhappy with her and would have done anything to move on, so we moved!

So finally we were moving to our own place. The excitement was out of this world something we did together. Well you can't destroy one family and expect just to continue on with yours, the proof was what to come. During his Terroristic Threat incarceration he blazed by with the skid of his teeth of no hard time thanks to her and connections she created.

Unfortunately, those favors didn't include him to be with me. Therefore, he didn't tell me of all that had happen I was just happy he was free. He tried to drink away the truth during our move. Oops, intoxication is a crime while driving! During the move he made his stops where the cans were as high as the seats of the u-haul. In the meanwhile again in the dark I tell him we have to return the truck.

He followed me safely and then I remembered I had to fill it back up with gas. He was told to go ahead I'll meet him back at the drop off spot. To my surprise I get back to him in the midst of an alcohol testing with the police. The quick talker I was, I tried to fast talk him out of this situation. The words stuck in my head how he said he would never go back alive. I by now had delivered our child who is now 6 months.

I continued to try and convince the officers that I will get him home safely and take full responsibility, obvious this wasn't our first predicament like this. This time it didn't work but the fact I had my baby while he got away for a drastic eluding of the officers, I was charged also! Obstruction of justice, charged and arrested, I had to protect my baby and call my dear friend. Please come to pick up the baby, hurry! Kenya had picked up the baby and drove him across state line to my sister to take the responsibility I couldn't take anymore under the circumstances.

I was so embarrassed and felt so innocent but when you look at a situation from the outside you may get a whole different concept. One being why was I with him after knowing he was married. One in earth did I think he was going to do to me after he abandoned his family. Most importantly, how can I face myself after knowing all the facts and not doing anything to end this mess ----"Selfish Love"!

That kind of love you can always believe and know it's best to leave it where it was. Sometimes we are to ignore our wants to do right by the maker. You're always safe, and secured when you follow that rules. Immaturity make takes us away from that time to time.

Challenge however will make you reflect back to what it is that should be done different. Challenge of motherhood, age or even the joy of reaping the benefits when done in a Godly way.

It always appears to ignore the right way and go into the temptation of what our wants are. The consequences are much larger than we can handle most of the time. The only time consequences shouldn't be considered is in our childhood when we are just finding out what that means. Even then it could be detrimental on your whole life aspect.

I can remember about 8 yrs of age myself, our molding ages. I had a best friend name Nicole and it wasn't anything I didn't share with her and her family. I probably was very annoying but the family never swayed me away. I remember when I took on her family as mine. There were cook outs, family gatherings, trips and even calling her mother mommy as I do till this day. You never know what effect you have on a child's life that is so young and vulnerable, try to make it as impressionable as you can.

I'm sure looking back now there were many problems with my adopted family, but I never was involved and neither were my friend and her sibling. I think "Mom" was a strong, private woman who kept it all separate from us. She allowed us to grow up with simplicity and innocence. Something I couldn't receive with my mother at all. The time I spent with Nicole was the time I would be running from my life or just needed to feel love of a family.

Everyone has that place or moment and they escaped to and feel right at home, that's called solace to the soul! I guess that's where Cherie ran to was the housing projects. I always kept a health environment of growth for my family. That was to boring for Cherie, I can only imagine the stories she had to tell that kept her interested and away from home. I can only touch on the basis.

Remember, we are going through the changes of childhood, puberty, womanhood, and into a relationship with your daughter. The only way to understand it all is to tell stories of our lives that may have connected us or taken us away from each other. It was my job as a mother to protect her, and her as a child not to know the difference besides to do whatever she wanted to do.

I lost Cherie when she couldn't accept the divorce and I continued to lose her to the change that she wasn't willing to take. She surrounded herself with negative friends and doing all that wasn't on my rule schedule. I was losing her but refuse to have her lost without me putting up a fight. Every rule she broke I had a consequence. The only thing I had on my side was the law.

Unfortunately, she wasn't breaking the law for a long time. It was just behavioral problems. In the midst of all this I had to tell her it was a possibility that in between me and her father's infidelities, she may had become a victim and not be her father's child. I didn't know for sure nothing but I wasn't going to raise her in the poor town that we were in and my way out had come when my husband and I decide to take me to my hometown. The rebellious stages had then started.

I had to deal with her dating at just 14 and tried to be open but yet stern. She was honest to bring her friend's home to meet me, but regardless of my opinion she was to see them. As she made her visits to the other side in the projects the drama she loved to be a part of she was dismissing my curfews. She was punished but I had to work and wasn't able to see that through.

I think my only controlling break through was her shoplifting, that finally got the "systems" –the law attention. Now I had fighting grounds, she was slapped on the wrist with probation for stealing the day I gave her cash to go to the mall. It was her destructive behavior that insisted on her doing something out of ordinary. I'm glad she had the taste of that behavior that seems to feed her!

So there was a point system within the probation. I used it to my advantage. I had a speed dial tone to her officer. Every time curfew wasn't met, every time she ran away, even every phone number was reported where she called me from. Her friends got tired of the police coming to their homes for her and she became an outcast. In the meanwhile her time was up and that what she had to serve –time-.

Before I had these options I tried exploring the run-a-way systems of homes and 4 of them were unsuccessful. They were never able to stay on top of her whereabouts to get out of there and run some more! Now that time had to be served, you can see the intelligence out of her. She portrayed a good kid in front of the judge. Yes sir, no sir, I understand. Good posture, eye contact all the works of a great con-artist!

Fortunately, my relationship with her probation officer kept me on top of the game she played! She was sent to an all-girl group home only 45 minutes outside of the house. Of course she didn't know it was so close. It gave visits together, picnics and other things that brought clarity to her madness. Her siblings were allowed to visit as well as long as she followed the rules. Look at that it took all that to get her to follow rules, something we all have to do in our lives.

Rules are made to put things in prospective and order not to cause us to be distraught. It should be an early lesson learned or part of the raising of all children. It should be in place and demanded to be followed; it is the beginning of preparing them for life.

Disappointments are easier handled when rules are in place to cover mishaps. If you break the rules know the consequences and are ready to accept them. That goes for both morally, and physical. Our moral breaking of the rules plays a part that takes a toll on our forever life. It's like the myth of breaking the mirror you get 7 years bad luck. Morally if you disobey some of the commandments you spend years trying to figure out how did you get where you are and where the time went.

The circles we chase ourselves in are inevitable when we keep making the same judgments in our lives. Cherie packed and left me at a time we needed to stick together as a family. I had struggled with some bad decisions I made in life that caused me to separate from my family, and as a result I packed for us all to get a fresh new start once again. I set them up in school, but we had to stay in the basement until I was able to get a place for us.

School was easy for all those who attended this small town high school. Although, Cherie founded easier to skip school, find a job, and pick and choose the path of her destruction. Her later consequence was teenage pregnancy. She thought she was grown and could handle it all. Cherie proceeded to play the role and shacked up without a second thought.

As that fell apart with the frustration of the lifestyle she wasn't use to with her companion, she returned home. Or should I say I had to pick her up after being informed she was totally destructive of the betrayal of her companion. She was forced with anger in behavior that could only lead behind bars. Again, as her protector I demanded she come with me home. I had by this time had a new place for us to live.

It was a new fresh start of life; I enrolled her in school and again put forth more rules to follow. She had my youngest child in her care while at home and I worked when she didn't. One of the rules was to work, get out every day and look! Continue education and make plans for her future. She traveled in her times but she was to remain within the boundaries I had set.

It was a refreshing time for our relationship. Her pregnancy of my first grand-child was exciting. I was actually glad she shared it with me. I went through the planning of his arrival and the lay- out of her plans. I at least thought she planned it with me. Later, of course I found out she had another agenda.

My rule was you can stay as long as you like, but once you leave no coming back. I was expecting her to take advantage of that, get her life in order. Instead, Cherie started communicating with an ex out of state. He promised the world so that they can be together. She felt safe with him since he was a part of her past. Once again dreaming of a family life as women, she fell for everything except marriage.

Childbirth to Cherie was an awakening of what she had put me through as a parent. She had devoured herself to me with tears, on how she appreciated my motherhood. I appreciate her as well she was a champ. She was brave, strong, mature and ready as she can be! Motherhood struck us both, as I stood there in tears seeing my grandchild born. I never experienced the other end and it made me appreciate that life was brought to me.

After she had relocated she found to be on cloud 9, as all beginning relationships were. This was different in the fact he took care of her and her child at only 3 months old. She didn't take my rules with her to be as independent as possible, so she fell in the hands of misconception through love. He was doing well for a while she didn't work or need for much, but she got comfortable and ungrateful.

As he felt weary of her ungratefulness, he became rude and in compassionate of her needs. He had now felt it was better to abandon her there, and leave her in his family's home. She didn't even communicate with me on how it happen or why, but just how she handled it. I received a call she was in a hotel, working and paying daily. A very vulnerable state when there was no one to support you. I did the best I could from long distance, but the most of the work needed to be by her!

Under no guidance besides her strength and determination, she made it on her own to her own apartment. It was motherhood, that had pushed and directed her to success of giving the best to her child she can. I was very proud! Cherie had learned that all she had was me, myself and I in the end. It was the tribulations that we experienced together to let her know that our lives is what brings us to the moments we cherish.

Feeling quite lonely while not being in a complete family – without a man –; she encountered her companion and allowed him back into her life. This time smarter than before with the tests of what he could handle without feeling distress and applying abandonment again. She made the call to me and said he was on his last foot and her heart would not allow her to leave him out when he was once there for her.

So first the test went on by being a woman by her man's side while he gained employment. Then it went to being patience as she continued to pay the bills by herself. Next it was, understanding that all he doesn't have to offer will come soon. Not final but the closing step, disappearing and coming in odd hours of the evening to soak in his sob stories. Absolutely, the final his appearance started to go with his actions and that is not acceptable!

Brings to the point of character! Character is a determination on which who you are. It is important as first impressions are. Be sure no matter how low you may feel that you look your best. I was told you represent me when you a couple, and how true that is. I would hope you are in order when you are with me as you are when you are not with me ---represent!

Of course we all have our more comfortable days, when we aren't here to profile but to just run a quick errand, but even then be remembered by your smile or gesture of respect. Something we must keep in mind as woman or man, you have one time to submit that first impression on whether you are of character to be tasteful or disgraceful. With that in mind we need to take heed when we are yearning to meet our other halves of a soul mate, give them the decency of being the best of you that represents who you are and what you stand for.

How do we begin to fight for our lives is what I want to talk about next. As a second grader I recall being chased home by three of my classmates. I was so scared I ran as fast as I can until I thought I was safely at home. What a surprise when my mother answered my call for help with a slap in my face. "If you don't stop ringing my doorbell like that", she yelled!

As my classmates were leaving they were called back to fight me one by one from my mother. Then she looked at me and said whoop their buts or I will whoop yours. At that point I was more scared then when I was running home. So I fought with all I had, I must have done well because the other two ran off. The point I'm making if you run scared from life it will always chase you rather than you living it.

Fight for what is important to you. Know what your values are and how to achieve your goals. Or life will just chase you into a drowning hole. If you were blessed to have children be sure your relationship with them are strong enough to carry you through whatever it may endure. Know that your blessings are counted and served when you can accomplish a respected relationship with your seeds.

The support you may look for in the opposite sex is usually right there in your reach in your children. Never let anything come in between that, but yet in still does not let them be the reason of unhappiness as well. If they are not for your happiness they may be what you would call a bad seed, something that needs to be replanted from the roots. Find that issue and try digging for the right soil to heal their soul, but not at your expense. We can only guide at that time.

When do we let go, when the respect is gone! If your child doesn't respect you let them go until they realize you are the parent and they are the child. NO matter what age, it all stands the same. My motto is don't love me, respect me and we will be fine. You should be able to raise your eyebrow and they know the reason why, without saying a word.

We see so much of ourselves in them sometime forget that they are to be chastised just as you were to be. How funny, there was really no one to give me a behind whooping except my mother. Even without, I knew I couldn't play with any of my fraternal family. As the words were spoken I will knock the "dailax" out of you, and that's what they meant! May not even be in the dictionary, but all of us knew what it meant.

I talked earlier about protecting my Cherie from herself, it's only right that I extend that a little more. After I had Donavan (my middle son) and going through the abandonment of his father, she became my hero. She kept him through the nights I barely had the energy to speak; she changed him and even fed him as hers. I figured as much as I pushed him on her she wouldn't be likely to have her own no time soon.

I had always worked hard to keep the children in good schools and great neighborhoods, which means lots of working! I worked as an accounting assistant by day; waitress and CNA by night on alternate days. Except on the weekends it was all three. You can only imagine the exhaustion I had. Cherie was the one to help me make it happen. She was great with the baby; of course he went to daycare while she was in school. Other than that she kept him and I tease her till this day on how he's her child.

My plans may have not worked accordingly, by I'm sure Cherie has stories on how she learned responsibility, independence and became mature quickly to adapt to her current life. Decision making was definitely made easier, not to mention what she taught me on how to be a better mother. I still would need her to budget the groceries. I only know how to get what I would desire; budgeting doesn't appear in my vocabulary.

I have told these stories to show motherhood, and the things that makes us stronger going through mishaps of relationships. In addition, I need to save a passage on just saying to those who are not yet mothers. Take your time in choosing your child's father; we have so many families separated because the time is not spent on getting to know our companions individually.

How do you actually know if he/she is right to be a parent of my new baby? Everyone has a shadow in the mirror that may reflect darkness. So it is always safe to go by a person's child rearing days. Respect is taught early in age by our parents, if that is in place we can pretty much go forward with interest. I always say don't love me, but respect me. Love is respect, know how to treat me, show me care, and provide for me and a path we shall walk together.

It is always safe to say that Male's relationships with their mothers are always a sign of growth as a man. A man is not to be taking lightly in word, demeanor or actions. A man is not to be proven or raised, he is to be looked at and know by his swagger as we call it that he stands in such form. We choose by the fact of the way they carry themselves as an individual, and we are to take place as his strong back bone.

We can't expect to have a strong man of gentle ways, strong errors if we are weak ourselves. Show him your strength by numbers of your child rearing of single mothers, or new mothers the ability to take on your responsibilities.

To gain out a great relationship, you must insist on being a brand of quality within yourselves.

In today's struggles it's even a bigger struggle to be a character within good quality and self-satisfaction. We have concerns with our family lives, our weight, finances and when we will be prefilled with what brings us happiness. Therefore, let's try and get a handle on the way it should be handled –in my opinion, in which my experience gives me the authority.

I had the ability to screw my life over with the wrong decisions of choosing those to share my life with. This is why I can take my time to school you on the time I had wasted not listening to others in hoping this reach someone and take an affect over change in their lives. Love yourself more than anyone else; never delay your life for a companion. If they don't come to you as a well put together individual pretty much that means now they are going to waste the both of you time not just theirs!

My last child was brought into this world on the blind love I could have endured. I met him and he was sexy, cute and quiet, so I was interested. It was a routine of going to college to shoot the breeze and holler at this individual who did nothing but catch the eye. I had to meet him and persuade him to learn from me and be who I wanted him to be.

He had a deeper secret of himself then I could have ever imagined. He was a true alcoholic; at first while getting to know him it seemed normal. We would laugh, drink together, and ever be amazed by each other. I cooked, cleaned and introduce him to my child as someone I felt to be special... Then it was apparent that the behavior was there I just chose to ignore it because I was determined to try something different and not just look at my finances to be enhanced.

The conversations to himself got longer and longer, then to his ex-wife, who warned me he may be Bi-polar; my thought was she could just be jealous. He was most of the time in place, he teased me with little finance he offered for Thanksgiving dinner and getting my hair done. I thought that was a considerate gesture to prove he was genuine.

He was a working man; I would send him off with his lunch and prepare his daily dinners, thinking I was getting a winner. My first hint should have been, when he was told his mother was in an accident that he didn't know where she lived at. Remember, what I said earlier good man have good solid relationships with their mothers, he didn't even know where his lived!

Back up to the ex-wife who stated he was bi-polar and my response was her to be jealous. Our most definite mistake is not to listen to the ex, no don't have a regular conversation and relationship, but do listen and have an open mind. It's not just jealousy if they are not lying about the facts in your face. Sometimes, they want them to meet someone else just to leave them alone…sounds familiar!

Past relationships of our companions are important as well. I can mostly have a cordial conversation with my ex that can be pertained in an open environment. I would trust we don't hate each other, or want to see ill of each other. There are other instances where relationships where the individuals can't be in the same room without drama and despair from hate of each other from what the other did, now that's cause for concern.

To continue on my journey as a misguided individual, I felt all these signs were not important. I didn't take them as warnings as they should have been, I only ignored the facts. I was so determined to make a family with who I had, not knowing that I was missing a very important source "A man". He was still growing upon himself and I was only an enabler to make him think all was good the way I accepted all that he did.

I ignored the fact that he practically allowed me to go homeless, and I had to bounce back on my own and into his promises. He promised a new place after I packed and moved out of state for a new start, just to miss his misguidance of what I thought was love. I came back probably weaker than I left since I continued to accept his lack of providing, for my family.

He didn't have love but he spoke of it, this is why we don't go by words but actions. I had all the time to think to get rid of him because his actions showed no respect or love. Instead, my needy self decided to play dumb and get deeper in with the mess. After he lost his job by incarceration for a dispute we had, bringing upon return all the jailhouse promises of becoming better.

I was impregnated and great thought I believed that he wanted to be a part of it. So he went off to rehab and after two months insisted on returning. He returned not only back into my household but back to his old habits of being a drunk. My younger son wasn't quite ready to give up on him yet at this time. He wanted me to give him another chance to prove his-self, I took that as a plus that he built sometime of bond with him.

Now I know his hope of having a father figure around is what he wanted. He was of course a child of confusion. After months of the fighting and terrorism of us fighting through the whole pregnancy he was then completed and directed away from having such tension around.

His decision to not believe him anymore was my decision of giving this last chance. It was then I found he betrayed me in the worst way. It was only the friction but now he broke the only bond we had (sexual) by sleeping with someone else and letting me find out about it. Totally not acceptable, I know I'm too good of a woman to share with anyone and I will not with no one!

It was the most hurtful thing, first to find that there actually was someone. Then it was going through her lies for him and his excusing her. It was almost was as if I was losing my mind, because my heart knew but I wanted to believe his detailed betrayal. I didn't want it to be true so I convinced myself to believe him. Finally, it was the obvious and the anger began.

You never want to give him (the one you love) up to someone else. Therefore, I came to agreement to try and forget. It was kind of hard when every night before climbing in bed with you he called her to say good night. Maybe, it was the fact that she forwarded a message from him saying he loved her that did the trick! Of course she never admitted it was a relationship until she realized he wouldn't be back to her. Except the evening he was on her porch with our son! As a woman we must believe our intuition and do not place it elsewhere for the convenience of playing fool!

It was like he was justifying himself because he got incarcerated for doing me harm, and I didn't stand by him that he was expected to go elsewhere. It would have been fine if he would have done it before tying me back in emotionally. We were separated 6 months with the last three months no contact. The next mention heard, was he had a job to start and needed funds to bail out. I donated my amount from my son's schooling for him to be able to better himself.

Of course, it was all family lies to protect his dirt on what he wanted to do----GET OUT; by any expense! The mention of her would anger me so much, especially after finding out that same family was well aware of it all going down. Don't ever think that you are a part of the family because they are his (her) family regardless of what dirt he does.

I found later she was at a family gathering with him and me, and even held my baby all a part of the betrayal I felt so deep in my heart. It hurt me so deep when it was time to let go I did it with ease. Once trust fled a relationship there is no easing back into it without drama. I felt he wasn't worth the drama nor my time or tears!

I only wish that I would have made the decision before bearing a child, falling in love or not being able to escape the stalking I acquired now! I wanted so much to believe people can be good if you show them good. It is all within them if change is to be made not in what someone else does in that person life. No matter how much you take the mule to the water stubbornness always take effect until otherwise realized.

Never accommodate your emotional needs with being physically disabled to yourself growing into someone bigger and better than you are. When you allow someone in your life that is a disabler to the progress of your self-satisfaction or empowerment of being all that you can be than you are taking away the gift God has given you. He makes no junk and we will not allow anything in our way to become junk.

Your dreams are your lifestyle, you are to live as if you already achieved so you may know to count your blessings at all times. I feel there is much too much of garbage that is stopping my blessings. If you hold on to the things that hurt you in the past it will continue to hurt you-----LET IT GO!

It is just a barrier over you when you hold onto luggage. You could never move on and find what is deserving of your inner self where the good lie within the core. You continuously run from the pain that holds you down. To let yourself be free to be the best you inside you have to unload the troubles and brisk those off to the Almighty, his shoulders are a lot bigger than yours!

Barriers comes in barrels it's our ways to overcome and jump the hurdles. In the relationship hurdles, whether companion, sibling or child, be sure to accept what you must and separate what you would not. As a mother, I feel it is impossible to be a friend and while mothering. The confusion comes much later when not expected. If the whole time you raised your child as a friend you can't switch at the end when they become keeping you on the level as there friend.

However, I demand my child to respect me and to know the difference for all that she recalled I did for her presence as a mother. The demand includes to give unto me as I did unto her. I always provided and looked after her health. I love her unconditionally and she beared two beautiful grandchildren that I can share that love with and for that I'm grateful

I hope in raising her children she keeps in mind all I lacked in my parenthood and become that better parent. It was hard at times for me to show the love or the passion because of the lacking I had in my raising from my mother. I always had love in my heart but I was always built to be strong therefore sometimes love isn't expressed as it should towards my children.

All my siblings I believe do not have that expression of intimate love with their children. It's a exterior of being tough and to be sure we don't have any weakness in our children as we were taught. When you grow up around fighting and arguments it brings a lack of respect for love. Infidelities, betrayal and things that taught us to be withdrawn, were the reasons that started early in our lives.

Protection of each other was another strong attributes, we were to never let anyone hurt our family members. Wrong or right they are family and no one will harm us with the other of us in presence. Definitely it kept our family reputation strong. However, it didn't do much for our concept of the law. That was a lesson to be learned individually at our own concept reception.

That same concept it was have most of our males in prison. We were taught more to fight than to love. Although, it was our elders that taught us "God", and one thing we all know for sure there is a higher power! I think that what kept us humane. To think of all the times my mother had me in battle with her against others was utterly insane!

I think it was my mother's pain that made her angry with the world and she saw no other way but to fight. She fought with my grandfather, her husband and the world for not being what she wanted to be. What was expected of her and demanded of her. "She was smart as a whip but dump as a mule", my grandfather replied.

Yes, it's a different between the two; stupid you can't help being so, dumb you choose to be! He only wanted her to be what he knew she could but she never put forward the effort to complete anything. It was an easy road for her to travel only. If it wasn't easy she didn't get it! She didn't educate herself because it took time. She didn't become a nourishing mother because it took time. She didn't even take marriage seriously because he took her time from being herself as she was beat by him.

I just thank God I was given loving grandparents to show me otherwise, there is a struggle but the fight is yours when you are trying to achieve what you believe is for you. I was given goals young, I knew I didn't want to be my Mom; the destruction that she built for herself was not for me. I insisted not to be addicted to no drugs that can kill me and take me away from my family.

In my last words of this chapter I would like to relay to Cherie, my one and only daughter who inspired me to write this portion of my memoir. For all that I may have slacked in my raising of you be sure not to add it to our little angel's (my granddaughter) bag of luggage. Take what I didn't enhance in you and be sure to inspire her with it and understand the difference of being a mother and a friend! Know what you must instill and what you must omit to give a healthy, loving caring environment that will teach her ways of confidence and complete prosperity.

I have always taught "God" first and put your fears behind him and education to fill those heads with what would successful tools in what we call life which are full of lessons. The key is to be sure you live life and don't let life control you. Live life with assurance that the decisions you make will be fruitful and a blessing to others. When contributing blessings your blessings will fall as The Almighty see fit.

One of our favorite sayings is "He's not always within your time but always right on time!" These words are to live by because our blessings comes as fit for our way of living that encourages good when we do good, and bad when we're doing bad. It is such an easier road of less headaches and worries when we learn that although it is easier to do bad it is healthier to do the good that we were blessed to submit with!

Time of Tears

There are the many types of different childhoods and rising of boyz to men. As a woman I can't begin to write on all of them. However, as a mother of three sons I can at least ponder on the thought on how men become who they are. Currently, I have a Middle-Schooler whom is very aggressive. His type of behavior is due to the anger of not having his father in his life. He would never admit such or may not even realize how it all affected him.

His father was sentenced to 12 years when he was only 6 months old. He had been blessed to be released at 6 years and was able to rejoin with his son. For about a year in a half he had the notion being a good Dad may get me back on board. He was paying minimum child support and making visitation for about the same time, "Then", he found out I was involved. Out the window Fatherhood went!

Somehow new relationships to those who has an inferior complex means they don't have to support their child. It's left to the new man to be responsible for their child….. in a sick mind! His blood, his child, his responsibility just abandoned by the ignorance of inferiority…..if he doesn't have control of what he wants its easier to just leave it all. His childhood was with a step father whom betrayed his mother and after he told her she didn't believe him. He felt like a throw away since that incident as he defended her honor and she just pushed him away.

The experience left him feeling distraught since they were very close and even angry in many ways, but he couldn't bring his self to be mad at her. At that point he was on a warpath with woman...all of them. He couldn't be monogamous nor respectful, just suave and full of game.

That anger had him enlist into the Marines and destroy his self, because his basis hasn't been what a boy needed to be nourished as a man – Dishonorably Discharged. It is just a case of childhood of a boy destroying the character of a man. Childhood is a main element of a healthy respectful man. It is his character, wellbeing and response in a relationship that is started upon such.

A boy who has been neglected by parents abused, rejected, and constantly ridiculed usually ends in a controlling background. If he loses controls of anything it counts against him. Before gaining control though, there is the self-esteem, identity, and feeling of worth that is pardoned upon.

There is an escape needed in between childhood and becoming an adult. What route is taken? Great, to find that security within someone or something that makes them feel whole as a man. I myself had always been the nourishing type so it's easy to find such security within me.

One of my exes would be the one to say he didn't love me just knew I was strong enough to get him out of his situation and on to better and bigger things. Love came later, after he found love within himself. He had to know he was whole by himself and feel the love from others that will be a reflection of what he felt to be real.

This meant many affairs and reassurance of what behavior is accepted. He felt that once he found identity in his women then and only then was when he could be at whole. So he thought, in reality he just became confused. He grew up in a home where there was always two heads of household, and it was instilled in him that's the way it should be. He wasn't happy with his situation of marriage, father and provider.

The situation was just comfort of knowing he had a place within. He was much more comfortable in a state of confusion which why he couldn't be faithful, trying to run a business that only fit as a cover to stray, and of course just to provide for the children and have no activities in there lives besides the yelling of what to do and not to do. He wanted all to fit until it was not tolerated anymore! Reality kicked in that separately wasn't his best mode just made him more dangerous to him with an open lifestyle.

Then it was the responsibility to have the kids visit and it would be all fixed he still had the title of a good father. Of course long story short he remarried in about three years, that's who he was! I promised not to write this book on trying to be a man but just by experience of those around me and who or what they represented.

I'm hoping you find yourself in one of these scenarios and recognize what can make you the better man of your life. You have a gentleman that was molested and fight with the fact that he knows he's a man and not a queer. So he's tough, got to be hard, be looked upon as the man, or even take an occupation to push authority onto others so they can reflect back on what they were made to do and be safe with it.

Pain is from within and can't be conflicted upon others without hurting yourself. Emotionally it is a wound of mental health that needs professional help and you will prove to be stronger to face it as such. To put a face to every man's inside can be one of horror, joy or surprise.

As a man you are taught to be strong, emotionless, and not to tell your feelings. Connect the dots and realize, especially as an African American man you are the lead in heart attacks and strokes just by that reason. Know when to tell the difference of expressing your feelings or damaging your manhood.

Desperation is another part that takes place when you're unable to make it a point in your life to be weak, full of emotion and honest about the way you feel. It is the most attractive when a man access such personality.

You ever wonder why the queers and woman love to be in the company of each other. They like the emotional attachment where expressions are not held back and the thought of sharing the innermost experiences with a true friend.

It is a wonderful thing to have that in your mate and yet he's so masculine and able to protect you and love you as well as treat you like a Queen. It is within his manhood to know his self and relate to the inner feminine side without feeling out of place.

Let's talk about being in a more disadvantaged neighborhood where you look up and you're no where but down. I personally feel those that come out of such places with good mothers are the most heartfelt men you can be surrounded by.

They know the advantage of making what you have work, the respect of a woman who makes the most of what is giving, and most important they see others who don't have good mothers taking the route they don't want to go. It gives them more strength, strive, and indulgence to become the best of what they put out for success and blessings.

However, the wrong route, let's see no mentors, no positive influences, not even uncles or fathers that they can reflect with because they all are incarcerated, dead or on drugs. For these gentlemen, there is always education that can help them rise or if that's not in the family history try what is known to you as a skill.

Taking the young ones that think taking of things that not theirs may be able to go for a trade as automotive, or the graffiti artists as a painter, and there are always the illegal pharmacists that become technicians. Place yourselves in positive thoughts on what can be changed rather than concentrating on what is blocking your way. There is nothing kool about being a fool. I like to say think of the dream of what you want and awake yourself in it!

Probably you're right it is easier being a bad Azz but you know anything worth having isn't easy to get. Don't overwhelm yourself with every obstacle that may be in your way but make plans to eliminate one by one with diligence. Most to remember when things go sour please don't feel someone owes you something because it didn't give a sweet grape. If you're not working find a McDonalds, Wal-Mart,

Burger King whatever so employment that will bring a paycheck. It definitely beats a blank!

If your criminal record that you may have blemished yourself with slows you down, then take the classes offered to better yourself in these situations so there is documentation that you have tried all you can. Even then if you still don't find yourself in that dream you keep on looking for that skill within you because the Lord doesn't make any junk! Persistence and endurance is the answer to most problems or the lack of trying something new if one thing doesn't work.

When all else fails and you find yourself bored nothing to do to intercept your confusion or bad habits then find a place where you know you can make someone smile without the temptations of trouble. One prayer I put out is it doesn't take a death or your death to make a change in your lifestyle, if you love anyone do it for them until you learn to love yourself with that important step to make a difference and to continue in whatever got you there!

A few good times you have moments where the household is a solid foundation and there are no criminals in your immediate vicinity and yet you continue to follow the thugs' right to condemnation of your own doing. You think your mature people of your surroundings got it easy never had problems, issues, or just lucky. No..!

They kept the idea in their head they never wanted to see inside of a jail or institution fear was their issue. They feared not to be surrounded by their families, their loved ones or even the ones they admired that wouldn't tolerate such behavior since they were looked at as responsible and reliable people, because of their character that led them to where they stand today.

Fatherless Son

Daddy? I am becoming a man..where are you?
Got the girls in school at Me, who to choose?
Growing hairs on my body, bad news?
Personal hygiene, body odors, Im confused.
Dick getting hard for no reason..not a clue
Daddy? Where are you?
Can you see me becoming a man?
Do you understand?
Mommy can not teach me to be a man.
I need you..I seek a plan.
She said to respect the females but for what?
I see why with Mom, reason to respect her,
Beyond much.
To hold, love and nurture her? My lady
Says I dont know of such.
I say Ive learned to with Mom..yet still Dad
How to love & respect her? I have nothing but to
Assume.
A fatherless son hurting and asking still
Daddy, where are you?

So don't take for granted your family that is giving a good example or showing at least a comfortable lifestyle of sanity and peace. Take heed and follow their steps! My question is what makes men act the way they do when out of order....here is my answer the woman of their lives. Whether an abusive mother, an unloving woman that they loved or a sister that showed hate during times it should've been an understanding they needed.

That being said, here is to the strong sisters that contribute to the good men in the world. Always treat everyone the way you want to be treated and under prayer and grace you will find it is more of a blessing to have been received than a problem of despair. We always as women need to look around at ourselves and our actions to our young men brothers, boyfriends, sons etc. and know that we affect our men in ways we will never imagine.

A man of true character in which we admire is one of a list that has been created long before we demand them in our lives. Let's see how well we settle for what we get rather than what we want. When I first started dating it was plutonic, then my little heart started to pound harder when I saw Mr. B is what I will call him. The pound was love but of course as many do you can't love the one you with you love the one who loves you.

Settling! Starting from the beginning of many of our lives we can see how we are redeemed to settling to what we think is best rather than what we want. As a little girl I settled to let my mother run in and out of my life which I was to young to understand that was abandonment. As I got older and my father was deceased I only prayed that I will find someone that can reflect his part in my life.

You see the fairy tales and place yourself within but in reality, those are stories of someone experiences. On point of men reflecting behaviors of women and becoming who they are. Read my pattern, Father, brother, boyfriend or the fellas. They all think upon what has been taught to them by action or by words. As strong women we are what they eat! Show them our weaknesses they take that as advantage to show our strength they want that as they're backbone.

To discuss more of the men I have come across. The strong person, that has gave up his desire to be gotten by any woman again. Had a family, children, house, pick-it fence and the dog. Divorce took it all away, so now he shares the attitude of many, I will never put myself in that situation again!

One year later meets a young lady that he adore but still have the wall up and she will allow him to do as he please with their relationship. As long as he not led to commitment he will continue to go with ease the way things are. She has settle to think this is what she wants and she is unaware that her emotional ties are only going to get greater on her side only.

A character of a man is built on the type of man he has grown into. I applaud providers that are confident and connected with the Lord! This will allow his convictions to be guided with sound reminders of what should be. It is however our job as women to make those reminders consequences of what will or will not be tolerated.

I want to introduce a few fellas that deserve a line in two from what they taught me or what I know of them. Let's take the first five that comes to mind that I will give a character. First, here is Seymour's story. He was born two a married couple that had the sequences of a strong family. He (father) was a man who believed to take care of his family and to be strong in values. Father taught to be settled in your shoes, not to be weak or distressed by what we may call struggles. She (mother) was dedicated, strong in Jesus and respectful to her family with love. And as they say the Lord takes his angels into his bosoms early for that's where the good souls lay. Mother was diagnosed with cancer when Seymour was 12 years of age. That brought Father into despair of someone two take care of him and his brother. When Seymour turned 18 he joined the Army and went into the service knowing that he wanted the same lifestyle for himself with security. After four years of service he came into town with one intention to find a wife. Seymour was such a strong character that he would only be attracted to a submissive woman. One who shows to be unsure of herself, and needed or wanted to lean on someone she can depend on. Of course beauty still had to be within, a heart of gold. So here goes Abby, a lady of grace and strength. Abby was strong just coming back from an abandoned relationship of a prior marriage. She had to swing into survival for her children; she was sent to town with a bus ticket and two small children in her lap a few diapers and a little bit of money that may have lasted for the rest of the week. Abby felt tired, alone and disgusted as her abandonment became her struggle from being able to care for her children. Her husband was more obligated to other woman and liquor whichever one would get in his hand first. Therefore, when Abby saw Seymour in his uniform walking behind her as she was leaving the store she was flattered and hoped that he could have been someone she can confide in and understand her struggle. Seymour was a loud mouth as you may call him, pretty blunt of what he wanted and how he was to put in action his plan. His plan was to find a wife and to be able to take care of her as well as give her what she wanted. Abby just moved in with her aunt in which was very strict on dating or anything that will blemish a woman's name. Seymour sent a few flirtatious comments as he hummed behind Abby. Stating he was on a look out for some good company. Abby was more quiet and uninviting to the idea of a man chasing her. However, she needed a friend. They courted (way back) on the porch to get acquainted and in no time at all once Abby expressed her concern the gentlemen stood up in her honor. He put a plan in order for her and the children to have residence before she knew it he gave her the details. Of course with the state Abby's mind was, she didn't believe him but with contact to be only by phone and a few visits in three months everything was in order. Seymour had kept his word and was sure to have the family on its way by giving peace and security. They later married and moved in together. That took a man to know what he wants how he was going to get it and inspiration to continue with such dedication. A man of character we would like to duplicate and box for most women. Where did that old fashion courtship go? and the respect of family and what makes a family stronger without expectation. When something of such magnitude grows around us we want what we know and see. That was the foundation that we grew strength, dignity, anticipation and love. He knew nothing about Abby but yet it was her warmth, heart, and content of what she shared with him that made him love her and know what he wanted for someone. It led to a marriage of many years and appreciation of the children that didn't know where their father was or even what he was doing to care for them. Seymour didn't care who, what or when someone was going to step up for these children he did what he had to make it right. Abby was open to his suggestions and it lead her to be able to care for her family. She didn't stop in his tracks; we are made to be strong from birth as woman. Instead, she took that a time to expand her efforts. Abby found a job and learn to make money as well. Together they stood fast on what was needed. She later had two more children for Seymour and he bought a brand new home after working at his new job and disciplining himself to save for what he felt was a part of being good to his family. It was the beginning to show what was important as a family and how to derive from nothing to something with love and determination. Seymour worked as a chauffer and became successful of what he found as a trade and made it a career into his own small business. Always able to keep focus on educating the children and keeping them with what was needed as he was as distanced as a father could be. He was what you call the provider, Abby put in many hours at home and at work to be sure that the family was flourished with essentials. That story was to get most to determined and assessed how life can be made into cherries with the right motivation and intent. I'm sure when Abby found Seymour or he found her she didn't think he had the potential to be what they were that day. Instead she had in her head how her first husband left her and had no concern of caring for the children as a man should as a provider. The difference between Seymour and him was that one had better intentions, hopes and dreams than the other or at least the thought being put to action rather than concentrating on the stumbles and obstacles that kept him her first husband from doing what he needed to be successful to what he had committed to do. Act as a husband as his vows stated. This is the action we can only hope to be taken when you are the one on the other end of a relationship. Unfortunately, when men only thinking with one head in these generations; we as women don't receive such respect. I want to bring the attention to another time of life when a couple met and it was a moment of true love at first site if you believe in that. It started as a blind date, but right away after the man asked what exactly does she want in a relationship he sold her a dream based on what she needed. A strong male model for her previous children, to be stable, loved and adored, along with the possibility of a long term relationship that will turn into a marriage of success. As he was selling her these dreams, she had no idea that he was already married with four children and no intent of keeping none of his promises. They started there date at a family picnic with his job, she felt it was a special place to start on their new journey. Then he took her on a shopping spree to her favorite places. First, they shared their common interests of what type of living space they wanted and then the taste in furniture as well as the special interest in art he displayed. Then they went out to eat and have drinks before going to a movie. A day of bliss is what she thought she was having. In the end he had abandoned his family and gave his paycheck towards this dishonor to his family in search of something new. Not until 4 months down the line did she realize it was all a lie. Emotions had been exploded within this four month period of time, and it was never his truth that brought things to light. It was a phone call from one of the children that she had answered to express his where about. Later, the phone call from the wife herself in which during this conversation was that she was still married to him and they were only in confusion at that time. His explanation for all the constant phone calls was he was behind on child support and was trying to catch up. Of course with the finale of him asking to commit on one knee was what she thought to be romantic. Now let's think on what would make a man do such damage as an individual to another. He has to be emotionally disturbed to pretend on a whole other life just bringing disgust to his family. He ignored the calls for help for mortgage payments, child care, and the care of all household responsibilities. In addition, not to mention she had met the children on which she thought was a visitation allowed by the mother (wife). He was going to work normally, making mends with the wife while returning to the home with the new girlfriend as if all was in order. He had convinced the girlfriend they had been separated for months and that the divorce was already in process. In the meanwhile he had convinced the wife he wanted a new beginning. He was to relocate to assist in a family business and be able to support the family from afar until he returned. He took the girlfriend on this new relocation stating he was hoping to rid himself of the drama and be able to commence to becoming independent enough to support his children without the extra of his wife's nuisances. Two different stories and same man of deceit to both women caused an uphill of distractions and layers of lies. The girlfriend watched him for nights of sweats, bad dreams as well as claiming that he needed his children closely to him and expressed he wanted to bear another child. Confused, to the situation and being naïve to the real deceit she became pregnant. This relocation was a disaster to all involved peace was no closer than from the beginning of this error. Later it was disclosed it was the wife's family business and she was a pawn on the table at this point. They returned to face the music and it all blew up! He was sent to jail for terroristic threats against the wife after he found she had started a relationship as well. The whole pregnancy was shared from the jail walls and bypassing of the wife. Then the day of release come forth while both women waited. A moment of truth or deceit came to be questioned. He went home with one woman and returned the next day to the other, with the excuse he needed to get some personal items for work before leaving for good. Did she when a prize, absolutely not. She inherited his problems of insufficiency that led to his incarceration. A man of uncertainty on how to deal with his problems, is to be unsure of which he had done was abandonment in the worst way to his family as a disgrace. Only to abandon the new family he tried to inherit. A military background that failed, upon the dishonorable discharge that was sentenced to his life because of the terrible temper he had. It was an excuse for all only in his mind. Promote womanhood and create manhood something in those lines as "Judge Joe Brown" states. Why is it so hard for men to state the truth......because they are lying to themselves in most cases? A man trusted to leave his family for months at a time for work. Is he worthy or totally in dishonor to his family? He starts relationships each time he separates himself from his family. Only to leave her with heartache, despair and loneliness behind as his lies and stories piles up against the truth. Does he even have the honor to tell of his family, of course not? The other woman thinks she is in a growing relationship hoping that something of the future will be inspired. Of course he constantly states that there isn't room in his life for a relationship so it is all in the actions that are deceiving. The words used are to protect him from being the liar he is. I have a son's mother whom I'm not in love with but love because she's the mother of my child. He spends time with the other woman's family, stay many nights sharing times of trouble laughs and enjoyment of his choice. However, its just slipping the ole word in we're just friends that keeps him safe from his actions. Waking up early mornings in each other's presence, his family even sees the possible of a growing relationship as she drives him to work and answers his needed call of requests. Movies, dinners, breakfasts and all the activities of a couple and the impression there is no other in the picture not at lease during this time period. The magic words "Friends" takes away all the responsibility of making it what it is or even to think the possibility. Unfortunately, that only work with robots. No human of emotions is going to fall for such explanation without being deterred into a different direction mentally. When the smoke clears and he actually returns to his family all the way to that point it was the stories on how he would be living with his sister, mother, or whomever he can find temporary living arrangements. Since prior he states there was no relationship with his child's mother they were long separated before he returned for work. In addition, during their courtship it was two women he was involved with so what would make the other woman think there was anything in her way of becoming his mate. All the games within a man are titled by their own actions. When they finally man up is usually when they're caught in the B.S. that they have to make excuses for. Then there are the suave men that know they have it going on. Good job, personality, bank account and potentially a good husband profile. All of that confidence usually leads to control and eagerness to be proven of some detail to them in which are in a form of demand. With the shortage of women to men ratio they feel they have that right. However, sisters we fall in the category of having it all too but yet they call us stuck up and names for our justification on knowing what we want and our worth. Especially, which whom have aggressive personalities. We're to strong, we talk too much, and most of all we never listen to them. As an African American woman it is in our generations of such attitude. Although as any other nationalities there is the other woman within all of us. The one who lets their guard down and decide this person we will trust until they give a reason not too. Brick wall girls, is what I call the personalities that don't trust see good nor even appreciate someone who cares. Eventually, that wall has to come down and will be intimidated by the patience and the understanding of those who care enough to take the time within your well being. The time to show they will be there even when the days aren't good between us. Rain, snow or sleet I got your back and I will never lay on it and do nothing. I hurt when you hurt, I laugh when you laugh and when you are the one to question my character and doubt my love I will be the one to look the other way until we see eye to eye. You get to the point where there is some things just not worth fighting over, the small things that can make me smile the bigger things that shows my blessings and most of it all the things that make my life worth more than an argument but of substance, appreciation, endurance love and Great Spirituality. It's always that ticking clock of age that prepares us of change. It's something about men when they hit Forty, and women in there Thirties. Our goals come shining in our face when age would come upon us. I should of, could of, would of, and what if. In reality, our goals are the character we build and the morals we live by is what makes our lives. Personalities, daily ways of our actions and the way we even think will be the effect by which we stand. Going to work every day for many is what our blessings are but yet we should know that we work hard as we will live forever but don't forget to Praise our Lord as if we will die tomorrow. In daily inspirations, it should be of top priority. As a high time of our peaks, it should be a time of praise and worship, because every step of the way has been by the comforting of our Maker. At our lowest point we praise him! Now along the way is where we have the problem, the in between is the journey. The journey of learning is our place in this life, to be lived in a story worth telling. Starting a travel of such is of many paths, where are we going, what are we doing and how we get there. To know it all is the beginning, the path to knowing is to be aware of ourselves. At what point are we of our lives that we live as a job application states are we entry-level, non-management but experienced or management. Our most pains and hurts stands to be the experiences by which we are made stronger or weaker. The tears we cry should be the motivation to carry us and the pain we feel is just the act by which the strength the Lord gives us that we know is not more than we can bear. If you are young and under 23 it will be most of entry-level to most, to channel such pain or hurt can be a little harder since the experience isn't there. Therefore, it would be led by the teachings we have received by those in our elder. Listen to those who has experienced and led by the fact that we lead by our morals and character that are created within a very young age that we call responsibility. When young and in training our parents for those who were fortune enough to experience, tells us our step by step process of getting ready for the day. Brush your teeth, make your bed, wash your face, wring your washcloth out and tie your shoes. When too young to appreciate the guidance we call it a daily nuisance for the most of our mother's words constantly repeating themselves on a regular basis. That repeat is the guidance of consistency and the respect of receiving it is how we start our obedience by which we accept authority. We grow from small those steps, in which life to us, the actual factor of time when you're rushing around in the morning getting ready for school. Did you remember your homework? Do you have a sweeter on? Remember to turn your report in. The reminders that we take advantage of from our parents are even expected in our time of childhood. One day you send out no reminders or small morning talk and things are forgotten or misplaced, guess that they turn to (smile). You didn't remind me Ma, I heard many times. It is occurred as an expectation rather than a reminder. This is how we graduate from stage to stage from the responsibility by which we take into our own hands. Are you entry-level or non-management but experienced? Did you just blame your actions of disappointment on your past or a person in your life? It was your mother fault for not teaching or telling, your aunt that you were raised by or just the person who loved you enough to speak of your downfalls and to discipline your actions. Our maturity plays a large part of our character or morality that is displayed with action to accept or deny. As an adult all excuses of our childhood are dismissed and shouldn't be dismayed as an interior motive on stand- by of why you did or said what you said in harm of your being as a responsible person. Being in many conversations on daily basis you hear so much of when I was a child my parent always did this or that so I thought it was okay that I did it too. It is only fortunate when you use their good work habits, and use excellent communication skills, pass on their special skill sets in home and family. We can't take their lack of success in as our down fall on why we can't reach our goals. They have their reasoning and now you must use your own. In that fact there is no excuse for failure besides not trying. We must know to try first and take our failures as steps to complete our tasks of success. In experience when I failed it was because I didn't have the ambition to complete or the aspiration to inspire to completion. Then I found my biggest cheerleader is myself! If I don't push myself on or inspire myself by the completion of my accomplishments no one will. Greatest attempt in which to reach success in life knows the balance of life and personal that will be an influence in a positive way. You reach out to the positive people in your life, don't be drained by the lighter influences that drag you down with their drama, help but don't enable behavior that won't have them acknowledge their weakness to be handled with care. In addition, there is a fine line between happiness and acceptance of what is tolerable. Find your happiness in your ways of life that may appear to be in sync with what we have accepted. Find time to laugh, grow, expect the little things and demand the things that still make you blush. I have been called goofy many times but I have found as long as my laugh isn't hurting anyone I will continually do so in full intense. It doesn't hurt to smile once in a while as well. Never allow your heart to over take your sense of reality it can only lead in despair a place you don't want to visit. If you ever feel like you're to giddy, feeling childish and careless but yet you're a grown up then change gears! You may not be in the right place in your life when you have to adjust more of who you are and your mindset than usual. We must also recognize there are seasons in our life for more reasons than we expect. The people we meet, the reasons we talk, the time we are discussing such topics as timing of events in our lives and mostly those who affect us at a time or moment we never expect. Some moments we step back and feel like we are on a fast track even for ourselves to keep up then all of a sudden you're sick, weak, and disgusted for reasons unknown. That was the moment for you to be still look back and see where you been and where you are now. It is hopefully a change for better and a time of experience you may need to explore a little more on why you have reached that point. When you know the difference in the median of taking a break, slowing down or taking time that's when we have reached the Management level. It's not the degree that leads the managers, it's the knowledge of knowing how to handle the ways of putting things in perspective of whether it will be family, career, money or even decisions that affect many lives under your umbrella as we say in the corporate world. The many umbrellas to be assessed into a precise direction of a percentage on what areas are handled, at what timing is in the best interest of the family. I wonder if there is a way to put life in a cut clear way of handling the issues, dramas, concerns and affiliations into how we handle it all. I think to start with a prayer and end in a prayer is our most clear way of understanding. For those who are not religious at whole God help you! After that's settled then there is within the emotions of what we conclude as important in our lives. Some feel it's their looks, some may say it's their weight but most of us go for love, whether we love ourselves, looking to love or awaiting a special love in our lives. Upon losing a close friend who always asked me whether he was going be a part of this book, I want to express the time of confusion, despair, and hope. He is already a part of this book but I wasn't going to let him know but he has affected my life to be worth a few words. I had hoped to be able to get the connection with someone, mentally as we shared. The despair of wishing there is someone abroad as such and the confusion on how I was unable to express I was awaiting him to pull it all together so things will move forward in a different direction for us. However, he is gone and now I would never be able to express. I feel sometimes people are taking out of our lives to reflect on exactly what is it we are seeking. There are some good honest, trustworthy and loyal brothers abroad. As woman we need to reflect on ourselves on perhaps a daily basis are we ready for someone with such qualities to enter our lives. Are we ready to receive, give ourselves as a whole and love as one? It is a tough spot to mentally put yourself in but it must be answered before wasting someone's time energy and well-being of opening themselves up to you. To receive you must be able to give without hesitation neither doubts of trust. It is so hard to open ourselves of in such ways but it takes work on both sides. When you organize your clothes or your tools or anything of worth to you, how do you reflect? Which way you want it to be done at a way to be convenient to you, easy for you, and attractive of by which will appeal to you. The same as in relationships you are to take that same important reflection but to know nothing is easy without preparation. Preparation starts from within, to know which steps you are to take which way you are going and how to get there. I had a conversation with a young sister who was in love and about to have a child but yet was already bored in the relationship. The relationship had just found commitment to living with each other and moving to a safe neighborhood by which they wanted to raise their child. I spoke to her in the manner of if you are already bored and it's just starting; where would the relationship lead? It is up to her as a woman to make the interest, constantly changing means there is no time for boredom. Rather in the decorating of the house, the diversity in the meals the planning of the weekends, it is to be explored as one and intertwined as two! It is the knowing of what one likes and to expand the grounds by which you tread. The purpose of this final chapter is to educate the boyz by which they should become men. It's not about the ones who don't feel that a woman can't show a boy to become a man but the ones with knowledge to realize that a woman knows a good man by which she chooses when being a good woman. Looking for that match by whom she can share her most intimate secrets and not be judged but for him to nurture and to understand the feelings that makes her feel weak but he makes her strong. I think of all the woman that says they don't need a man when all they are crying is they refuse to accept less then what will combine with them the matter by which they call success. Success isn't always by the income that we receive but by the prosperity our lives blossom. The man that is secure within his-self enough to know his weakness allow his faults and admit his shortcomings. By which of all he rises above and become that provider of the soul the hard-worker of the household and the back of the weak to whom needs his shoulder! I think of the step fathers of those who were fatherless and gained the respect of them from childhood to adulthood. He used his wisdom of teachings his love of no judgment and the patience to overcome the fear of the child that helped them gain as a family and not just some rascal sticking their head in for such a short period. Then you can't forget the hurt souls of the children who don't trust or want to love or even look at the future because they're so hurt from their past. The single mothers can teach and tell and usually come with some very strong young men and women but their always a missing void because by the word of the bible it takes two to raise a child. True men love with their heart and feel with their soul without the hesitation of fear of hurt because they know as they grow further into the relationship and what doesn't appear to be compatible can be left and put behind as the future becomes a different path. We carry so much baggage and if the trash isn't put out we can't do anything but carry it and it outweighs anything of purpose. The reasoning of our being to be blessed or stressed comes from the choices we make that will allow us to grow or to be hindered by our relationships. Hindrances are things that should be sought out and arranged in an order that we can delete permanently. Sometimes things need to be dealt with in category. As which I will not allow my past to dictate my future, I will not have my enemies become greater than me because of the effect they want to have over me, and for sure, I will demand of my future to be better than what it was because I am of greatness by which the power of the Almighty gave me! The way these issues are attacked is first to know of them and then to relay to that Devil land under my feet as I stomp away the awe of all that interfere with who I'm becoming. It is upon relationships of life that you find the ones that are healthy and promising and others that may neglect you in every way. Find that neglect to be barriers of something of a greater extent! I found that I had obstacles within me around me and above me but when I take it to the altar I can leave it and know that my Almighty has taken care of it by which time will tell me how to deal with it and be sure it doesn't stop me now or ever. Personalities come in many forms that need to be dissected into many parts. This world deals with each of them in their own ways I was once told that if you want people to take you serious than you can't smile laugh giggle so much those who know me understands that's like a root canal. It's not being taking serious but being able to adapt to your environment accordingly. I work in a very strict environment of a class of Accountants and my laughter drives them crazy but I'm not to bring a smile to your day always….good in Sales but not Accounting. These differences in such actions are detail enough to effect income and stability that I haven't quite reached yet but it is on my Ace card to be topped of all else. That said to make a point know where you're going and where you're coming from to make the impact by which you need to overcome obstacles, hindrances as well as enemies sometimes they are the ones to motivate you, you know what we cause those are our "Haters"! Life is always by which you make it and don't take those words lightly. It takes hard work to build a person of character and to avoid the temptations of wrong and ignore the paths of destructions. Making it means to become who you choose not what is chosen for you, you are your ancestors and the sweat they dripped the whips they took and gave either it is to be known by which we live now is in making of simplicity compared to the descendants by which we became. Brings me to a thought of how our current generations don't know the meaning of how to make it happen! We are so wrapped up on who is holding us down and the system working against us and how our personal opinions interrupt our growth. Taking the other descents that combine their incomes in a home to reach a goal by the 10's. The family sits and states what the goals are and who or what percentage comes from individuals of the clan. Individually we can't be as strong together we are over powering if we discipline our wants of the finer things such as cars, luxury of restaurants, traveling, extravagant gifts to ourselves. Know that instead we should be thinking what we leave behind to our seeds of life and our footprints to be left behind. Teach morality in what is the elaboration of success by which we pass on for our children so they can be blessed in abundance. Instead of blaming those who are more fortune than us by which they work hard and overcame obstacles of their life. Let's be blessed to teach and testify on our blessings! I came from a background where it wasn't what I had but what my family had, I had to work for mine and still set out to be sure all of my seeds are sewn in success by the power of themselves. Power within the education, struggle of knowing how to place what it is on the grid that you have to dismiss to be where and what you want. Want more for yourself than your parents or guardians want for you, those who love us always have destinations that we are usually to stubborn to follow. Instead of the energy of being stubborn and misplaced in our anger or lives step out on your path to destiny by the word and knowledge of the word we are to be plentiful by which we want, need and expect! In Jesus' name I demand that all of which take this book in hand will be overflowing in the joys of happiness by abundance in prosperity and the true meaning of what's to come when we are disciplined with obedience! I want the brothers by which I speak of in this content to grow as fathers, providers, strong shoulders that they imagined to be broad and thick for the woman that stand by their sides through thick, thin and otherwise. I foresee women to raise the boyz into strong men by example of morals, religion, and keep only positive role models in their lives. When we are broken by our men let them go when are men don't compliment us they shall be gone and if by any chance they are not providing by which the values of our wishes as a team are not met they should be on their path of condemnation! We are not to be doormats but to be wise enough to be ready when they need a push or a shoulder to lean on for comfort by which they have given you by terms of the household they have followed and if not joining in a venture of your family then point them in the direction to make a change without abandonment but do not let them be of hindrance to our mind body or souls because we are Queens holding on to our Kings but everybody isn't ready to enter the kingdom! Most of times we take what we had in previous relationships and just pass it on to the next and there hasn't been no work put in to deserve such treatment. We must be at a point where if we choose to have someone join our destiny they are to be worthy! Broken men who are still stuck on what isn't working for them because of the excuses they have made relevant to be as they are and not to grow stronger, better nor valuable to society as the man they were put on earth to be, shall not prosper. In all honesty if you can't pair to overcome and you have been forthcoming to receive failure, denial, and cursed with your own insecurities then your effortless ways are of merit. I can admit and even will allow society doesn't easily accept our African American men with faults and it is that fight that may take more than most. However, you are too look inside and find that one thing that no one knows or sees but you and make it shine…..This little light of mine I'm going to let it shine." When taking on consequences of trouble that you find yourself into and think you are that one that won't get scorned by life itself, you use that same energy to turn it around into the positive that must be made through you because failure is not an option. There is a need for you on this earth and you are to find it excel with it and overwhelm yourself with the efforts to make it what it should be your life shall be claimed not excused! The prisons are filled with those who have given up over and over again and not behind the bars that contain them and hold them but even within they find that one light that must shine. Your destination is based on your need of acceptance and purpose. I feel when using tenacity to complete your worth you will be of conclusion to yourself that you will feel whole. Hurdle over all obstacles so that you will find the solution by which will bring you contentment and allow all those who love to be blissfully proud of what you made within your desolation. As men you feel like when things aren't going your way at the time you wish and the circumstances by which you have claimed it is wrong within the universe on what is working for you that means it's all against you. This is the time you are to step up and claim your own personal disclaimer that allow you to remove the negative work hard towards what is to be by the destiny of your life. Take your seeds of children that may not be in the path you expected for them to follow and lay the path through your actions of integrity, morality and despair to make change. Our weaknesses maybe just the key we need to overcome what is holding you back as well as the ability to lay out the facts by desire, knowledge and upcoming of what is to come.

Her

Working 3 jobs 2 children..she taught independence.
"Pray through the storm"
I was told to get through it.
Clean up my house.
To be nasty, a choice? Not it
If your bathroom and kitchen is dirty,
Not worse than your scent.
Be strong, God takes care of the children and fools.
She wasnt perfect. I embraced her heart and spirit to have not learned.
The hustle in Her sustains in Me.
At heart still I catch the early worm.

We are selfish sometimes in the element of what is best for us. When you are responsible for others or others hold you high in their being it's just not the deed to live. We are purposed by our love ones. They love us for who we are, where we stand in their lives, and how we will influence them. Influences are by far not to take lightly. Leadership of when, where, how certainly takes a main role. Therefore, when finding the impression to leave understand it is by example and force of the unknown. You may not know the answer to how, when, or where but it is your duty to find that change and make it work. Trust in the Lord of his destination he has written for you and pray for the guidance that will succeed in the direction of where you need to be. Sometimes we find we are at the wrong place at the right time. Our intentions usually are in effect with our actions. Intentionally, you want to meet the opportunity that will change your life but then it may have been an act of wickedness that may have deceived us and turned your head. We are to take control of what we want, think and make happen and only we can indulge in the encounters to express accomplishment. This chapter was to educate, inform and make our men stronger of what they had not made happen but yet excused why it hasn't come to pass. Listen to our elders they have been there and advice as such is delicate also important to the experiences they have been through which gives them the ability to explain with keenness! I feel all of those under my supervision failed to believe I had been there done that and decided to achieve a hard lesson of life. It is not by chance that you can be of success and within destiny by lessons given or knowledge taken. The ole sayings of our elderly hard head make soft a**, or don't count it before you have it, even don't put the horse before the saddle and many more. They were said for the sole purposes of our survival in life and the intent that we will use it not to demise but to lengthen our result of happiness. To know love ones or special others is to know and love ourselves and that partakes in being good to ourselves. Claim our fate by becoming what makes us happy, not the jobs of just income and security but as the ones who refine what we will be! Find the job that makes you happy and you will be successful in all that you choose to pursuit. Do not be selfish in your ways strong in your weaknesses nor not mindful of your faults and you will find the hunt of life to be enchanting. When looking for love find it in yourself and the confidence of you will be foot printed by the man of your soul. Soul mates comes in many different shades, personalities, backgrounds and what we discover in them is more of what we see in ourselves. Our family history and background may differ from our soul mates but our hearts will lead us to one another. Know your expectations stick to them and the one who loves you will expect to do even more to bring happiness to two as one! We fall short sometimes and lose our value by which we allow others around us to do the same, if you don't know your worth don't expect others to keep track. I love a man and he loves me is that enough....?? Most of the time it takes much more to enhance the relationship, that's the fun part. Are you loving through the hard and difficult times as well as the easy travels of growing on one another? Love comes with the good, bad, and shade through it all you should be loving to one another when you feel bad the other should make you feel good even if just with a smile. You should never feel obligated to make the other happy but have the need to want them to be happy because it's LOVE. When struggles appear it should be one hand washing the other on how to be sure you are both above water together. Sinking together isn't an option that's selfish love and usually shares the accommodation of someone not doing their part. The ole saying you can do badly by your self is just that! Together it should be a rise in all things challenged whether financial, assets, or just simple goals of the future. A RISE! It that can't be met together and you find you probably do more by yourself than switch….you don't have that partner. If the relationship compliment your weaknesses by showing you a path of how to direct better decisions then you are probably with the right person whom you can love to the end!

CPSIA information can be obtained at www.ICGtesting.com
Printed in the USA
BVOW04s0437010916

460666BV00001B/3/P